"I'm A Lawman."

Matt's terminology struck a discordant note in Virginia's mind. Lawman? The last time she'd heard the expression was in a Western film she'd watched on TV. "Umm, that explains everything."

"Sure." He grinned. "Besides, I'm feeling much better. The grub did the trick."

Grub. Virginia shook her head, but asked, "Then you enjoyed your meal?"

"That was the best Christmas dinner I've had since I left home."

Virginia was suddenly alert. "When was that?"

"Eighteen seventy-one."

His words, his phrasing, instilled a tremor inside Virginia. She had the eerie sensation that something was terribly wrong. She gave Matt an imploring look.

"Please don't start that nonsense again."

"It's not nonsense to me. I know when I was born, I know when I left home, and I know that I was ambushed on Christmas Eve, 1889!"

Virginia's sigh said volumes about her growing sense of frustration. Matthew Hawk was *certain* that he was from another place and time....

Dear Reader:

Happy Holidays from all of us at Silhouette Books. And since it *is* the holiday season, we've planned an extra special month at Silhouette Desire. Think of it as our present to you, the readers.

To start with, we have December's *Man of the Month*, who comes in the tantalizing form of Tad Jackson in Ann Major's *Wilderness Child*. This book ties into the Children of Destiny series, but Tad's story also stands on its own. Believe me, Tad's a man you'd *love* to find under your Christmas tree.

And what would December be without a Christmas book? We have a terrific one—*Christmas Stranger* by Joan Hohl. After you've read it, I'm sure you'll understand why I say this is a truly timeless love story.

Next, don't miss book one of Celeste Hamilton's trilogy, Aunt Eugenia's Treasures. *The Diamond's Sparkle* is just the first of three priceless love stories. Look for *Ruby Fire* and *Hidden Pearl* in February and April of 1990.

Finally, some wonderful news: the *Man of the Month* will be continued through 1990! We just couldn't resist bringing you one more year of these stunning men. In the upcoming months you'll be seeing brand-new *Man of the Month* books by Elizabeth Lowell, Annette Broadrick and Diana Palmer—just to name a few. Barbara Boswell will make her Silhouette Desire debut with her man. I'll be keeping you updated....

Before I go, I want to wish all of our readers a very Happy Holiday. See you next year!

Lucia Macro
Senior Editor

JOAN HOHL

CHRISTMAS STRANGER

SILHOUETTE *Desire*

Published by Silhouette Books New York

America's Publisher of Contemporary Romance

SILHOUETTE BOOKS
300 East 42nd St., New York, N.Y. 10017

ISBN: 0-373-05540-4

First Silhouette Books printing December 1989

Printed in the U.S.A.

JOAN HOHL,

a Gemini and an inveterate daydreamer, says she always has her head in the clouds. An avid reader all her life, she discovered romances about ten years ago. "And as soon as I read one," she confessed, "I was hooked." Now an extremely prolific author, she is thrilled to be getting paid for doing exactly what she loves best.

For
Parris Afton Bonds—

Who understands
that though we can never really know,
we can dream of all the wondrous possibilities

Prologue

Montana Christmas Eve, 1889

The snow fell soundlessly through the cold of the winter night. Drifting flakes shimmered in the light cast from the window of a small, isolated cabin near the edge of town. Inside the cabin, a man stood peering into a cracked, wavy mirror, muttering to himself as he raked his long fingers through his unruly, silver-sprinkled dark hair.

"Needs shearing." United States Marshal Matthew Hawk grimaced at his distorted reflection. "Needs washing, too." His thin lips twisted in distaste, Matt wiped the sheen of oil from his fingertips onto the threadbare towel he had moments before tossed onto the washstand.

Critically narrowing his eyes, he stepped back to get

a partial view of his tall, rangy form. The sight was not one to ease the frown from his brow.

Not new to begin with, his jacket was deeply creased from being rolled up inside a tarp and tied behind the saddle. His one decent pair of pants was in the same condition. Matt had tried to smooth the wrinkles from the material with a damp towel; the results were less than he'd hoped for.

Matt shrugged and turned away from the mirror. If nothing else, his shirt, though worn, was clean and neatly pressed. The white shirt, along with his black string tie, at least gave the impression of respectability that Matt was striving for.

What did it matter, anyway? The thought brought a grim smile to Matt's lips. He was a stranger in this small, barely surviving mining town in the Anaconda Mountains of Montana. Except for the local sheriff and a few concerned citizens, nobody knew him. All the same, for reasons that weighed upon Matt's mind and conscience, suddenly it mattered.

It was Christmas Eve, and it mattered because he was going to church. He, Matthew Hawk, a hunter of men, the loner-lawman known as The Hawk to friends and foes alike, the cool, withdrawn man who hadn't been to church for over twenty years, was getting spruced up to attend the Christmas Eve service at the town's solitary, rough-hewn little house of worship.

Dipping his fingertips into the tiny pocket at his waist, Matt withdrew a round silver railroad watch. With a flick of his thumb he flipped open the lid. As if in prayer, the black hands lay together on the six. It was six-thirty. Church services were scheduled for seven. It wouldn't take him more than ten minutes to climb the low hill from the cabin to the church. Sighing, he snapped the lid shut and slipped the watch back into its pocket.

What to do for twenty minutes? A new frown tugging his dark brows together, Matt glanced around the small room, searching for something to occupy the time. The room contained nothing of interest—just a rusted metal bed with sagging springs, a lumpy mattress and a threadbare blanket. Also a table and two chairs, none of them matching, all of them nearing collapse. Over there was the warped washstand, trembling beneath the weight of a chipped pitcher and washbowl. And on the rough wooden floor lay a handmade rag rug, which had probably been ugly even when it was new, way back when.

A sigh of acceptance whispering through his lips, Matt began pacing the floor and gave in to the unwelcome thoughts that were tapping at the back door of his mind.

He had killed a man less than twenty-four hours ago, and he had done it with cool, professional deliberation.

Matt shivered in response to the wave of revulsion that washed through him at the memory. The fact that he had committed the act in the line of duty didn't negate his reaction to it. The fact that the man had been a particularly vicious outlaw didn't alleviate Matt's sense of unease, either. His work as a peace officer had been causing him a mounting dissatisfaction for some months, and lately the dissatisfaction had bordered on despair.

Pivoting at the washstand, Matt retraced his steps across the room. Distracted by his thoughts, he no longer noticed the shabby furnishings or the ugly rug that was bunching beneath his boots.

He was tired, but his weariness was more of the spirit than the flesh. He was tired of assignments like this last cne, which had sent him trailing an outlaw for close to a month from central Texas to the mountains of Montana. He was tired of sleeping with one eye open and forever watching his back. He was tired of the slaughter, of killing men who seemed more animal than human. The outlaw Matt had been forced to bring down the day before when the man refused to surrender had been such an animal.

Matt was thirty-five years old. He had spent ten of those years wearing a badge, tracking the lawless, protecting the law-abiding. He knew it wouldn't be too long before the passage of time began to work to his disadvantage. He knew that once he'd lost that fine sharp edge, his days on earth would very likely be numbered.

Matt was well acquainted with death. He had witnessed it countless times; more times than he cared to recollect. Death was never a pretty sight. Yet strangely, Matt felt no fear or anxiety about the very real possibility of his own demise. No, the driving force behind his growing despair was an awakening sense of the value of life . . . any and every life. And with each new assignment the knowledge was impressed upon him of how very precious the tenuous thread of life was . . . to every living creature.

For over a year now the feeling had been growing inside Matt, something that sickened him whenever he was faced with a situation ending with death by the gun.

But in a raw, untamed land, what other options were there other than six-gun law enforcement? Matt asked himself, raking a hand through his freshly smoothed hair. The law-abiding citizens had to be protected from the aberrants who chose to walk on the wild side. It always meant violence that—more often than not—resulted in death.

Matt was increasingly certain that there had to be a better way. But what that way might be eluded him. Maybe, in another time, another place...

"Damn," Matt muttered, breaking into his fruit-less musing. He needed answers, and all he could come up with was more questions. Frustration was a weight that was becoming too heavy to bear.

Was the mental torment the reason he had decided to attend the Christmas Eve church service? A wry smile flickered over Matt's compressed lips. He had to admit to himself that he had a lot of gall to seek so-lace in God's house after all these years.

But he was more than a lawman, Matt defended himself. He was a human being, a man with needs and longings and dreams like other men. He was tired of living on the back of a horse. He wanted a home of his own, a woman of his own—and yes, God willing—a child of his own.

Maybe it was time to quit, to end the slaughter, at least his participation in it. What he needed was a second chance, a new beginning, a decent life.

Since Matt had saved a large portion of his earn-ings, all paid in solid American gold coin, the first part of his dream, owning a small ranch, was within his grasp. On second thought, there was no "maybe" about the situation; it was definitely time for him to quit.

Reminded of the time, Matt again checked his watch. It was growing late, five minutes shy of seven. If he was going, the time was now. Hesitating, he absently repocketed the timepiece. It had been so long since he'd set foot inside a church. Would he be welcomed? Not by the townsfolk for sure, though Matt didn't give a damn what they thought. But would he be welcomed by the ultimate Boss?

His answer came as he recalled a scene from his youth, when he had sat squirming beside his mother on a hard church pew. How had the words gone? He couldn't remember all of them, but the ones he did remember offered comfort and certainty.

Come unto me, ye who are heavy laden, and I will give you rest.

Deciding that rest was surely the first of his needs, Matt shrugged into his woolen coat, settled his weathered Stetson low on his brow with a brisk tug, walked out of the cabin and into the gently falling snow. There wasn't a soul in sight. Concluding that all the good folk of the town were already congregated, he glanced up at the beckoning light that was streaming through the church windows. After pausing to flip up the wide collar on his coat, he began trudging up the hill. He was halfway to his destination when the shouted sound of his name broke the silence of the night.

"Hawk!"

Alarm splintered through Matt. Conditioned reflexes took over. He was moving before the echo of his name faded on the crisp air. His leg muscles flexing as he spun, Matt dropped to one knee, and his hand streaked to the pistol that had become almost a part of his right thigh. Even as his pistol cleared the leather holster, a rifle shot rang out, shattering the illusion of a blessed and peaceful night.

Matt's body jerked from the force of the bullet that slammed into his chest. His eyes wide with shock and amazement, he felt his hand jam the pistol back into the holster. Darkness swirled through his mind. Then he was falling forward, his motion so slow that his hat remained firmly in place when he crashed, face first, into the cold cushion of snow.

The shock of cold brought a moment of lucidity. He was going to die! The realization shuddered through his ebbing consciousness as assiduously as his life's blood was seeping through the material of his shirt. His breathing ragged, his teeth gritted, he shifted around until he was lying on his back. Now he no longer felt the biting cold or the snow. The flakes no longer melted on his rapidly chilling skin.

He was going to die. There would be no second chance, no new, decent life. No home. No woman of his own. No child. There would be nothing, an eternity of nothing.

His lips twisted into a wry grimace. This was not exactly the kind of rest he'd had in mind.

As from a far distance, he heard the sound of church bells. No! No! Matt protested in silent anguish. He couldn't die. The thought was like a flicker of light in the encroaching darkness. Not tonight, of all nights.

It was Christmas Eve, for God's sake!

One

The snow began to fall late in the afternoon of Christmas Eve, delighting the children and dismaying their parents. At first it was a gentle sprinkle of light, delicate flakes, but by midevening the storm front had pushed its way over the Pocono Mountains to unleash its fury upon the small town of Conifer, Pennsylvania. And by the time the churches pealed their bells at midnight to announce the arrival of Christmas, over six inches of the glittering white stuff blanketed the town.

Driving through the swirling cloud of snow was tricky, hazardous for the most alert motorist. Dr. Virginia Greyson, however, was tired, which made negotiating the roads even more harrowing.

It had been a long day for Virginia, beginning at seven that morning with the first of three surgeries.

She had seen patients in her offices until six that evening. After leaving the office complex, she'd had to rush home for a quick shower and change of clothes, then had dashed out again for a dinner engagement at seven-thirty.

When she rushed from her apartment, the snow was falling gently, creating a sparkling winter scene suitable to the season. She'd had no difficulty in driving to the secluded restaurant, which was the latest hot spot for the local professional group of doctors, lawyers and such. Though she herself was something of a loner, Virginia's date was a member in good standing of that select group.

At thirty-three, Richard Quinter was firmly entrenched among the elite of Conifer. A direct descendant of one of the town's founders, he was the only child and heir to the Quinter family fortune, the product of innumerable insurance and real estate sales. And, since he was a personable and handsome bachelor, Richard was also firmly entrenched as the prime catch of not only the town of Conifer but the county of Hunter.

By rights it should have been a pleasant, relaxing evening for Virginia. It was Christmas. Since she had scheduled a break for the holidays, she was free for ten days. The only notation on her calendar was an invitation for Christmas evening supper at the home of Richard's parents.

Virginia liked Richard. He was interesting and fun to be with. But this had been different from their previous dates. The tone of Richard's conversation had suddenly shifted from casual to serious. She frowned with annoyance as she recalled the most pointed of the remarks he had made during the course of the evening.

"I'm afraid driving conditions are going to get steadily worse," he'd said immediately after greeting her on her arrival at the restaurant. "I shouldn't have allowed you to drive out here. It would have been no trouble at all for me to run into your apartment to pick you up."

Virginia supposed that most, or at least many, women would have felt pleased by his concern—but she never had reacted to much of anything like most other women. She hadn't been pleased; what she'd felt was anger at his words. He shouldn't have allowed her to drive? Who was Richard to prevent her from doing anything?

But not wanting to start off the evening with an argument, Virginia hadn't bothered to correct him. As it turned out, her silence was a mistake. No sooner were they seated at their table when Richard further injured her sense of independence.

"I'll follow you home when we leave," he'd said, "to make sure you get there safely."

Virginia had bristled, but had managed to reply calmly enough. "That will not be necessary."

"But—" he had begun to protest.

She didn't allow him to finish. "Richard, I'm perfectly capable of driving myself home." He opened his mouth again to argue the point. Virginia distracted him by making a simple request. "Do you think I could have a glass of wine?"

Ever the gentleman, Richard hastened to grant her request by attracting the attention of their waiter. Afterward, Virginia had hoped that they might spend the evening discussing the usual trivialities that they had in common. But it quickly became obvious that Richard was set on a far different, even unsettling course.

His attitude had taken on a proprietary possessiveness that had set off warning bells inside her mind. Though Virginia liked Richard she was not in love with him. And by her choice they were not lovers. While she enjoyed his company, Virginia felt no inclination to deepen their relationship, either physically or emotionally.

She was thirty-one years old, used to her freedom and independence, and in no hurry at all to change the status quo. She was successful in her profession and financially secure, looking neither for love nor an affair. And right now she was anticipating a restful holiday, not an emotional game of hide-and-seek.

Now, at twelve twenty-seven on a snow-tossed Christmas morning, Virginia decided that the last thing she needed was involvement, with Richard or any other man.

Gripping the steering wheel, she gritted her teeth and drove her car at a crawl along the deserted streets. At an intersection she carefully eased the car into a right turn, and immediately revised her decision. Absolutely the last thing she needed on this particular Christmas morning was the disheartening sight of flashing blue and red lights atop two police cruisers that were diagonally parked midway along the street.

A fender bender or a serious accident? Virginia wondered, bringing the car to a stop a safe distance from the parked police vehicles. Either way, there was the definite possibility of someone having suffered an injury.

What to do? Should she back out to the intersection and continue home using a different route, stay where she was until a police officer waved her forward, or get out of her warm car, plough through the cold snow and offer medical assistance?

Her shoulders slumped as she contemplated her options. It took her all of ten seconds to reach a decision. Virginia was an excellent, very scrupulous physician. Unconscious of the habitual action, she raked slender fingers through the honey-blond waves that cascaded to her shoulders. Her own principles limited her options to one. She was a physician—end of inner struggle. Sighing, she pushed open her door and stepped into the biting wind. Flipping up the deep collar on her ankle-length coat, she sighed again, then began tramping through the snow.

With each step she took, visions of malpractice suits danced in Virginia's head.

Skirting the cruisers, she stepped into the glare of the car headlights. The harshly illuminated scene didn't fit the festive season at all. She recognized the four uniformed men standing in a semicircle. The smile of greeting that tilted her lips took on a downward curve as her glance settled upon the body of a man sprawled in the snow.

"Eve'n, Dr. Greyson." Patrolman Jeff Klein respectfully raised his gloved fingers to his cap.

Virginia gave a brief nod in response. "What have you got here, Jeff, hit-and-run?" she asked, noting the absence of another vehicle in the street as she moved toward the body.

"No." Jeff's frown and tone conveyed consternation. "We got a call about fifteen minutes ago from a couple of the residents." He jerked his head to indicate the lighted houses along the street. "They reported hearing rifle shots." He inclined his head. "When we got here, we found him." He grimaced. "He's got a bullet in his chest."

Virginia came to a halt beside the still form lying in the snow. "Who is he?"

"Lord knows." Jeff shrugged. "We searched him, but couldn't find a scrap of identification on him. All we found were a couple of things, a watch and a badge, all old looking, like antiques."

"Odd," Virginia murmured, shifting her gaze from the officer to the victim.

The man was dressed strangely, the garb Western, but in the style of an earlier time period. A dirty-gray Stetson cradled his head. The wide brim framed his face, throwing into relief the taut planes and sharp angles of his bone structure. He had a long, straight nose, high, slashing cheekbones and a firm jawline. His hair was as scruffy-looking as his hat, though the overlong, silver-streaked strands appeared healthy and vital, for all their obvious need of a good scrubbing with an industrial-strength shampoo.

A latter-day mountain man? she wondered, skimming a professional glance over his sprawled body. Her normally soft brown eyes widened slightly in shock as her gaze collided with the holstered pistol tied to the man's leanly muscled right thigh. A hunter of animals...and perhaps even men? Whichever, Virginia thought bleakly, it was a shame to see him lying there, so cold and still. The stranger had been a hand-some and virile-looking man.

The observation was wiped from her mind when her gaze next collided with the large, dark red stain that was soaking the outdated attire covering his broad chest. An odd sensation—a confusing mixture of de-feat and bereavement—settled in her heart at the sight of the gaping wound where the bullet had entered the right side of his chest, close to his broad shoulder. She did not know this man, yet Virginia felt a sudden, inexplicable need to weep for the senseless waste of his life.

He was cold, so cold. Pervasive tendrils of dark-ness clung to his consciousness as tenaciously as the chilling snowflakes clung to his skin and eyelashes. Was he dead? Matt asked himself, straining against the dark cloud that enveloped his mind. Was this fright-ening, cold-to-the-bone sensation death?

Matt experienced a deep, inner shiver. He felt no pain. Yet there was this creepy sense of anxiety and cold. For some reason, he had always felt that death was nothing more than a state of nothingness... warm nothingness. But he was cold, indeed more than cold....

The darkness dissipated slightly, dissolving into shades of gray. He was wet! And there was something else! At the outer edges of his consciousness he could hear voices!

Maybe he wasn't completely dead, Matt mused. Maybe he was hovering in some netherworld, some limbo between the sweetness of life and the nothing-ness of death.

The voices were coming nearer. He could hear different tones, several deep and masculine, one lighter, pleasant, female. There was a minute change in the grayness that numbed his mind, a partial clarity. Collecting his weak powers of concentration, Matt fought to discern the content and meaning in the blurred syllables spoken by those voices. The garbled sounds meshed, then separated. Slowly the words became distinct and penetrated his consciousness.

"He's got the coldest eyes I've ever seen," observed Patrolman Raymond Horsham.

Virginia shivered as she gazed down into the ice-blue eyes in question.

"Well, of course his eyes are cold," retorted Cal Singer, Raymond's partner. "He's dead."

Unable for some reason to wrench her gaze from the stranger's blank eyes, Virginia pulled off her gloves and sank to her knees in the snow beside his lifeless body. A confusing sense of hopelessness and weariness washed through her as she reached toward his throat to confirm the absence of a pulse.

"I'm not dead."

Blending with the impact of his oddly fascinating eyes, the whispery-rough sound of the stranger's voice induced a ripple of shock inside Virginia. Startled, she gasped and pulled back her hand. He was alive! She jumped to her feet even as her rattled senses assimilated the realization.

Without a thought for her own welfare, Virginia whipped off her full-length coat to cover him. She had no idea how long he had been lying there, exposed to the elements, but she knew he was in trauma and shock. Unmindful of the wet chill permeating her body, she dropped to her knees again to tuck the woolen garment around him, then once again raised a hand to his throat to take his pulse. His skin was cold to the touch, which made the sudden charge of heat that tingled up her arm to her shoulder all the more devastating.

Controlling an urge to pull back her hand again, Virginia forced herself to concentrate on the strong but erratic pulse at the base of his throat. Touching him, feeling his life throbbing against her fingers, gave Virginia the strangest sensation she'd ever experienced. Her mind went blank, and her mouth grew dry with the realization that her own hitherto regular pulse beat was modifying, merging with the rhythm of his.

What was this?

Momentarily frozen, Virginia stared down at the man. She didn't hear the ambulance come to a stop or the dying wail of its siren. Trembling, stunned by the power of her reaction to someone she'd never seen before, she watched as his eyelids slowly fell. When he opened them again an instant later, his eyes were clouded by confusion but focused. Now they were a riveting, vibrant diamond-bright blue.

"Then again, maybe I am." Matt wasn't aware of the faint, raspy sound of his own voice, or even of the fact that he'd spoken aloud. All his attention was centered on the face that seemed to be floating above him. He had to be dead, he decided in a removed-from-it-all haze. For surely that soft-eyed, beautiful face, illuminated by a golden aura, could only belong to an angel. "I'm dead and gone to heaven."

The sound of his voice pierced the odd bemusement that was clouding Virginia's senses and restored her good judgment. What in the world had possessed her? she chastised herself. This man was injured. He was bleeding. He needed immediate medical attention. Blinking to break the eerie allure of his stare, she turned her head at the sound of approaching footsteps. The arrival of the paramedics snapped back her professionalism.

"Ambulance chasing, Dr. Greyson?" one of the paramedics asked drolly. Both of the ambulance attendants knew her, of course. All the ambulance personnel knew her. Conifer General was a small hospital in a small mountain town; just about everybody knew everybody else.

Virginia didn't respond to the young man's wry question. Jolting upright, she stepped back, indicating the injured man with an impatient sweep of her arm. "Please hurry," she said in a brisk tone of authority. "This man has been shot in the chest, and he has lost a lot of blood."

Instantly the men were all business, proving the effectiveness of their training. Though she moved out of the way to give them space to do their work, Virginia observed the procedure with sharp-eyed intensity.

After immobilizing his head, the men carefully lifted the stranger onto the litter. When they moved him, he gave a deep grunt of pain, then lost consciousness.

His eyelashes were incredibly long.

The thought rocked Virginia like a physical blow, forcing her to clamp her lips to contain the gasp that leaped into her throat. Helpless against the welter of emotions that was whirling inside her, she stood staring down at the unconscious, defenseless man.

Even with the weapon tied to his thigh, he looked heartbreakingly vulnerable.

Compassion stirred. He couldn't die. She wouldn't let him die! Blinking to clear her suddenly blurred vision, Virginia glanced around, startled, when one of the men handed her her coat. Watching in silence as the attendants covered the injured man and strapped him securely to the litter, she sent out a fervent prayer for the stranger... and for guidance for her own operating skill.

Virginia shrugged into her coat as she walked beside the litter to the ambulance. A shiver trickled the length of her spine as she folded the garment around her. The sensation was one of enveloping warmth and safety, as if the coat retained not only the heat of the unknown man's body but the protective radiation of his strength. Yet she knew there had to be precious little warmth or strength remaining in that depleted body.

She didn't understand why something inside her was responding to this oddly dressed stranger; indeed, Virginia felt that she didn't want to know. In any case, there wasn't time to examine her feelings and reactions. She had work to do. Whether or not she was granted unseen guidance, that bullet had to come out of his chest.

"When you call in, tell the receptionist in Emergency to collect an OR crew for me," she said, turning to trudge through the snow to her car as the driver shut the ambulance's rear door. "I'll be right behind you."

The motion of the vehicle jolted Matt into a blurred state of semiconsciousness. Given a choice, he would have preferred to remain cocooned in the security of darkness. He wasn't quite as cold as before, but now he was aware of a burning pain in the vicinity of his chest and right shoulder. He'd have preferred the feeling of cold.

Matt was also aware of forward movement. The sensation confused him still further. The motion was too smooth, too even to be that of a wagon or buckboard. Yet he sensed that he was in some sort of conveyance.

But what form of conveyance could it be?

The question continued to tease him. He knew of no horse-drawn vehicle that afforded such a comfortable ride. Gathering his limited strength, Matt decided to open his eyes and investigate the situation. He swiftly discovered that deciding to open his eyes and actually doing so were two entirely different things.

His eyelids were heavy, as if lead-weighted. The most Matt could manage was a mere slitting of his eyelids. The effort was exhausting, and not worth the results. He could see very little. Either it was night, or he was partially blind. And the exercise was not only tiring, it was frustrating.

Where in hell was he?

Matt moved restlessly, painfully as the silent cry exploded inside his throbbing head.

"Hang on, buddy, we're almost there."

Matt grew still at the sound of the encouraging voice. Questions, all without discernible answers, tumbled through his mind.

They were almost where? And who were they? Who was speaking? Where in hell was he, anyway? And damn, why was his chest on fire? The final question sparked Matt's memory. For an instant he could feel again the bite of night air, experience the sensation of swirling snowflakes fluttering against his freshly shaved cheeks. Within that instant of clarity, Matt heard the resounding echo of a voice sharply calling his name.

"Hawk!"

Matt's body jerked. Once more he heard the church bells summoning the faithful, relived the shock of feeling the bullet slam into his chest, experienced anew the slow motion of his own body, sinking into the cushioning blanket of snow on the ground.

He had been shot . . . ambushed!

The realization shuddered through Matt's depleted body. And with that knowledge came a mind-numbing question.

Was he dead?

Blackness invaded Matt's consciousness, and the question remained unanswered.

Organized confusion. The phrase was the only way to describe the activity that ensued upon the arrival at the hospital of the ambulance and Virginia's car.

"What are his vital signs?" Virginia asked as she leaped from the car she'd brought to a jarring stop alongside the larger vehicle that had backed up to the Emergency entrance.

"He's hanging on," the young attendant replied without glancing away from the injured man. A note of wonder was in his brisk tone. "Don't ask me how, but he regained semiconsciousness for a moment. Looked to me as if he was trying to speak. The man must have the constitution of a war-horse."

Leaving her car door open, Virginia strode to the rear of the ambulance to oversee the patient's transferral from the vehicle to the hospital. "Outdoor type," she said, making a snap judgment on hearing the report of the man's obvious tenacity.

Her comment was accepted with a grunt of agreement; there were enough "outdoor types" in and around Conifer, every one of them tested, weathered and tough. That the breed died hard was not only a given but a point of pride with the area residents.

That exchange was the last bit of idle conversation Virginia was to engage in for some hours. She began issuing terse instructions the instant the automatic doors swept open, to reveal the hospital personnel waiting to move the injured man from the litter to a gurney. Bespeaking the esteem in which Virginia was held by her contemporaries, her instructions were followed immediately and efficiently, without question or doubt.

Unaware of the police car that had swept into the emergency area moments after her, Virginia spun around when a hand was laid on her shoulder, prepared to deliver a blistering admonition. She bit back her tirade on sight of the blue uniform, but her tone betrayed her impatience.

"Yes, Jeff, what is it?"

"I'll need some information for my report." Though the officer's tone was scrupulously polite, it held a note of adamancy.

"Information?" Virginia repeated in angry astonishment. "Jeff, the man is unconscious, barely alive."

"Well ... I know, but ..." His voice faltered as he met her direct, cool-eyed stare.

Relenting, she softened her forbidding expression and tone. "He's being prepped for surgery. If he lives, you'll get your information."

"And if he dies?"

Virginia felt sick at the very real possibility, but concealed her feelings behind a calm exterior. "Then I'm afraid you'll have a John Doe for your report."

"Right," Jeff agreed on a sigh.

Obeying her mounting sense of urgency, Virginia turned away. She had taken less than a half dozen steps when she was halted once again, this time by an anxious feminine voice.

"Dr. Greyson, wait!"

Suppressing an expletive, she whirled around. "Yes, what is it?" Virginia demanded of the harried-looking Emergency Room receptionist. The middle-aged woman came to an abrupt stop to keep from cannoning into her.

"Regulations. Admittance forms," the woman panted, rattling the papers she held clutched in one hand. "Your patient. I need some information."

Virginia's patience snapped and her temper flared. "I can't give you any information on my patient, because I have no information about him." She drew a breath, then went on with more control. "The man is wounded, dying. I must get him into surgery."

The woman looked flustered. "But, Doctor, the cost! Who will be responsible?"

"I will." Swinging away, Virginia strode down the corridor toward the elevators. Her set expression was all the warning necessary to discourage anyone else who might attempt to delay her progress.

Virginia arrived in the operating room to discover a crew scrubbed and waiting for her. A sense of satisfaction obliterated her irritation. Within minutes she had changed into sterile operating-room garb and was standing at the sink, scrubbing her hands and forearms.

"Where did you find your patient, Doctor," a drawling female voice asked from the doorway behind Virginia. "On a hoof dust and gunpowder Hollywood back lot?"

Startled, Virginia scraped the brush over her knuckles. Frowning, she glanced over her shoulder at the small woman standing in the doorway. "Are you trying to give me a heart attack, Sal?" she demanded.

The woman grinned with the easy familiarity of a long-standing friendship. Sally Wentworth was the head nurse in the intensive care unit, and the closest thing Virginia had to a best friend. Her small, fragile appearance was deceptive. Sally was a veritable powerhouse of energy and as resilient as tempered steel. She was also the best nurse Virginia had ever worked with.

"Sorry," Sal said, grinning unrepentantly. "I didn't mean to startle you. Curiosity got the better of me."

Virginia drew a blank. "Curiosity?" She scowled. "And what are you talking about—hoof dust and gunpowder?"

"Your patient." Sally moved her head to indicate the double doors leading into the operating room. "He looks like he just stepped off the set of a Western film."

"Oh! Yeah." Virginia resumed scrubbing. "The police found him lying in the street with a bullet in his chest."

"Interesting." Sal's comment was indicative of the woman's unflappable character. "Who is he?"

"I don't know." Virginia shrugged. "The police didn't find any identification on him."

"Do they have any idea who shot him?"

Virginia sighed. "As far as I know, they haven't got a clue. They received calls from several residents of the neighborhood who reported hearing gunshots."

"More and more interesting," Sal mused. "In fact, it's darned intriguing."

"I could manage to live without this particular type of intrigue." Virginia retorted.

"Do you think you'll be able to save him?"

Virginia ran her hands and arms under the hot water for a final rinse. "I'm going to give it my best," she said with grim determination.

Sal's smile was slow and confident. "In that case, I'll get busy preparing a bed for the cowboy."

Holding up her wet hands, Virginia smiled her gratitude for her friend's confidence in her ability. "In that case," she said, turning toward the double doors, "I suppose I had better get to work."

It was exactly 1:45 a.m. Christmas morning when Virginia drew a deep, steadying breath and stepped to the side of the man on the operating table.

Two

The angel was back.

Peering through remnants of anesthetically induced fog, Matt stared into the composed, beautiful face once more floating above him.

Questions crowded into his hazy mind. Where was he? Was he dead? Was he in heaven or hell?

How did he feel? What *did* he feel? His eyelids were heavy. Closing his eyes, Matt brought his limited powers of concentration to bear on his present condition. He felt...comfortable. There was no sensation of pain. He was neither too cold nor too warm. The conclusion appeared obvious. He had to be dead.

Curiosity overcame the weight on his eyelids. When he opened his eyes, the woman hovering above him smiled.

Must be in heaven, he decided. That serene and lovely face could not be a product of hell. An angel, pure and simple. His own guardian angel? Matt fervently hoped so, because he never wanted to lose sight of her.

"How are you feeling?"

Shock jolted through him at the soft sound of her voice, the compassion evident in her tone. Did angels speak? Had she spoken aloud, or had he only heard her inside his mind? He thought he had heard her with his ears, but . . . Matt blinked. What had she asked? Oh, yeah. How he was feeling.

"Strange." Matt hardly recognized the croaking sound of his own voice.

The angel's smile held understanding. "It's the anesthetic," she said. "It'll wear off soon."

Anesthetic? Confusion deepened in Matt's mind. What in he . . . heaven was this "anesthetic"?

The soft voice continued. "I imagine you're thirsty," it said.

In that instant Matt realized that his mouth and throat were very dry. "Yes," he answered, wondering how he could feel physical discomfort if his body was dead. Once again, her soft voice interrupted his distracted thoughts.

"Here, this will help."

A shiver slithered the length of his body when Matt felt her slip one hand beneath his head. She was touching him! Matt thought in stunned wonder. An angel was touching him! And her hand was soft and warm . . . and amazingly strong! Then a secondary consideration hit him. His body! He still had a body!

He still had feeling…something smooth and solid was being inserted between his lips!

"Slowly now, take just a sip or two."

Obeying her without conscious thought, Matt drew on the tubelike object. Cool water bathed his parched mouth and trickled down his throat. The moisture felt heavenly. Greedily he drew on the object again, and groaned in protest when it was gently removed from his pursed lips.

"Take it easy," the gentle voice cautioned. "That's enough for now. You may have more later."

Still thirsty, Matt longed to argue but didn't have the energy. Darkness began closing in on him. Feeling himself being drawn back into unconsciousness, he groped with one hand until he made contact with one of hers. Vaguely the thought occurred to him that she felt real, solid, physical. Exerting the last threads of consciousness, he murmured a raspy plea.

"Don't leave me."

"I won't," her answer whispered to him through the swirling darkness.

For over two hours, Virginia patiently sat on the uncomfortable chair placed alongside the stranger's bed. She had little choice in the matter; her hand was imprisoned within the steel-like grip of his rawboned fingers.

She was still sitting there, dozing fitfully, when Sal came to tell her that she was going off duty. Virginia came instantly alert with the feather-light touch on her shoulder. Her first thought was for her patient. Snapping up her head, she stared into his sleep-softened face.

"He's doing remarkably well."

A sigh eased from Virginia's throat at the hushed sound of Sal's voice. Glancing around, she gave her friend a wan smile. "I must have dropped off to sleep for a moment."

"Is it any wonder?" Sal observed, her tone understanding and compassionate. "How long has it been since you've been near your own apartment, let alone your bed?"

Virginia shrugged. "Somewhere around five yesterday morning...I think." She frowned. "That is, if it's now Christmas morning."

"It is." Concern as well as amusement tinged Sal's lowered voice.

"What time is it?" Virginia muttered through an unsuccessfully stifled yawn.

"Exactly 7:06:22."

Moving carefully so as not to disturb her patient, Virginia arched her spine to ease the cramped muscles in her back. "You on your way out?" she asked, raising her free hand to smother another yawn.

"Yes." Sal's smile held the warmth of friendship. "But I couldn't leave without wishing you a merry Christmas."

Virginia's drawn features softened. "Thanks, Sal. I wish you the same."

Sal laughed. "I don't believe I'm up to merry—I'm beat. I'll settle for peaceful." Her dark eyes probed Virginia's pale face. "And you look about ready to cave in. What you need is about ten hours of sleep."

"I'm okay," Virginia murmured. "I rested for an hour or so after the surgery on the cot in the doctor's lounge."

"Wonderful." Sal shook her head. "At any rate, Hopalong Skipspurs was doing pretty good when I made my rounds fifteen minutes ago."

Virginia's mouth curved into a wry smile at the realization that she had dozed through Sal's going-off-duty patient check. "Hopalong Skipspurs?"

"Yeah." Sal inclined her head toward the man in the bed. "His vital signs are good, and he is sleeping naturally. Why don't you leave him in the excellent care of the day crew and go home to bed?"

"Two reasons." Virginia displayed the first two fingers on her free hand. "Number one—" she wiggled her index finger "—I promised him I wouldn't leave." She wiggled her second finger. "And number two...he's got a death grip on my hand." She nodded her head to indicate the tanned, bony fingers tightly curled around her hand.

"So I see." Sal rolled her eyes. "Well, there's one consolation. I doubt that you'll be shackled much longer. I figure he'll be waking up soon."

"I sincerely hope so," Virginia drawled. "This chair is beginning to feel like a torture rack."

"Oh, I almost forgot!" Sal exclaimed. Making a half turn, she picked up a clipboard from the low cabinet beside the bed and thrust it into Virginia's hand. "Speaking about torture, I was asked to give you this."

It wasn't necessary for Virginia to look at the papers clipped to the board; she knew what they were. "Admittance forms," she muttered, heaving a tired-sounding sigh as she slid the board onto the foot of the bed.

"Regulations, Doctor."

Virginia grimaced. "You mean—a pain in the—"

"Here now," Sal interrupted, lips twitching with a grin. "Is that any way to talk?" She shook her head. "And on Christmas Day, too. Aren't you ashamed?"

"No," Virginia retorted. "Actually, I'm too tired to feel much of anything."

"I can relate to tired," Sal quipped, giving in to a yawn. "It's been a very long night, and I'm ready for bed." She leveled a stern look at Virginia. "And if you had any sense, you'd follow my example."

"I intend to," Virginia assured her, then qualified, "as soon as possible."

"Yeah, right." Sal looked unconvinced. "I hear the breakfast trays rattling down the hall, and if I know you, you'll probably still be here when the lunch trays are served, hovering over Ol' Smoking Guns there like a ministering angel."

Angel.

Like the annoying buzz of summer gnats, Matt had been hearing the indistinguishable murmur of voices for several seconds. The actual words being spoken hadn't registered in his mind, until the sound of that one word—angel.

Was she still there?

The question both tantalized and terrified Matt. He was almost afraid to open his eyes to see for himself if the beautiful blond angel was still with him...almost, but not altogether afraid.

He pried his eyelids open to a tentative slit. For a moment his sight was fuzzy, clouded. As his vision cleared, Matt saw a dark-haired woman dressed in white, murmuring a farewell and smiling as she turned and walked away.

Who was she? he wondered. Another angel? Confused, Matt kept his narrowed gaze fastened on the woman's back. As she drew near to a portal or door, another figure in white caught his attention. This one, a much taller female with gray hair, was carrying what appeared to be a serving tray of some kind, and she was walking toward him.

An old angel? Matt mused, forgetting the first, dark-haired woman. Maybe this older one was in charge—somewhat like a mother superior in a convent?

The woman smiled kindly at him as she passed by. Matt was working his stiff, dry lips to reciprocate when she spoke, startling all thoughts of a smile from his mind.

"Your patient's awake."

Patient! Awake? In that instant, Matt realized he was lying in a bed...and not on a fluffy cloud.

Were these ladies nursing angels? he wondered. Were there such things as nursing angels? And if he was dead, why would he need a nurse? And if he wasn't dead and gone to heaven...

Where in hell was he?

Matt moved with restless agitation. Pain exploded in the upper right side of his body. Damn, he...

"Well, hello there."

The soft, familiar voice froze everything in Matt except his eyes; they darted in the direction of the soothing sound. She was there, the soft-voiced, gentle angel, *his* angel, and she was bending over him, smiling at him.

"How are you feeling now?"

"My shoulder hurts," Matt answered, shocked at the weak, unsteady sound of his voice.

"I'm afraid it will for a few days." Her smile was gentle with commiseration. She tugged against the grip he had on her hand. "Could I have my hand back, please?"

"No." Matt tightened his hold on her, afraid she'd escape if he let go.

"But I need it," she said in a tone of infinite patience. "Please let go."

"What do you need it for?" he demanded with belligerent suspicion.

The angel laughed softly. The beguiling sound of her laughter stole his breath and drained the resistance from him. With reluctance Matt opened his hand, releasing hers.

"Thank you."

"You're welcome." Matt had no idea of the depth of disappointment revealed in his eyes as he voiced his fear. "Are you going to fly away now?"

Surprise flickered across her lovely face. "No, of course I'm not going to fly away. I'm going to examine you."

"Examine me!" Matt exclaimed in a hoarse croak, experiencing a sense of embarrassment and anticipation. "What do you mean, you're—?" He broke off, eyes narrowing, as she raised her hands to a tubular device draped around her neck. "What is that thing?"

"This?" The angel frowned as she inserted the ends of the device into her ears. "It's a stethoscope," she explained. "Surely you've seen one before?" Her eyebrows arched, her face frowning in puzzlement.

"No," he admitted. "What does it do?"

"It allows me to monitor your heartbeat," she said, demonstrating by placing a metal, disc-shaped thing at the other end of the tubes to his chest.

Matt shivered. "It's cold," he excused himself. "What do you hear?" he asked curiously.

"A good strong beat," she responded, sliding the disc to another section of his chest. "And your lungs are clear." Straightening, she smiled at him as she removed the device called a stethoscope from her ears. "In fact, you're doing better than expected. Are you comfortable?"

"I'm thirsty." Matt was suddenly aware of a surprising sensation of emptiness that confused him. Maybe he wasn't dead, after all. A man didn't have physical needs after death...did he? Everything about his situation was more than passing strange, he reflected, and then mentioned the need gnawing in his stomach. "And I'm hungry."

The angel's expression brightened. "That's an excellent sign. I'll give you some water, but I'm afraid you'll have to wait a little while for food. They'll be moving you soon."

"Moving me?" Matt felt a twinge of panic. Was he being banished from heaven...from her? Deciding to clarify his position, he went on, "Moving me to where, from where?" He frowned. "Where am I now?"

"Postop ICU." Though her response was prompt, it merely increased his confusion.

Matt could feel his expression go blank. What in Sam Hill was a postop ICU? "What is a postop ICU?" he asked.

"Postoperative intensive care unit," she answered. "You're in a hospital...where you underwent surgery five hours ago to remove a bullet from your chest."

The mention of the word "bullet" brought memory slamming into Matt's mind as forcefully as the actual slug had slammed into his body.

Hawk!

The echo of a harsh voice calling his name ricocheted inside his head. Matt suddenly recalled that it had been Christmas Eve. It was snowing. The welcoming light of hope and redemption was beaming from the long narrow windows in the church at the crest of the hill. He had been walking toward that light, that promise of hope, when the call had shattered the night silence. A shot had rung out.

He'd been bushwhacked!

Reliving the incident, Matt slid his right hand to his thigh, wincing as pain streaked up his arm and across his chest. He ignored the pain when he realized his thigh was naked. His gun was gone! Suspicion crawled through him. Somebody had taken his weapon. Without the piece he was vulnerable. He would be unable to defend himself. Eyelids narrowing over eyes suddenly cold and deadly, he sliced a look at the woman.

"Where is it?" His voice had gained strength, and was as cold and deadly as his eyes.

The woman appeared genuinely perplexed. "I don't understand. Where is...what?"

"My gun."

"Oh, that." She moved her shoulders in a delicate shudder. "It's with the rest of your things which, I assure you," she hastened to add, "will be returned to you."

Robbed of the question he was about to ask, Matt grunted in response. His mind was becoming clearer, sharper, as the lingering effects of the sedation dissipated. He was becoming aware of his surroundings, of himself. "What in hell is this thing?" His hand moved from his thigh to the tube fastened to the back of his left hand.

"Don't touch the IV!" The woman's hand grasped his to pull it away. "And don't strain your right arm. You could reopen that wound."

Matt's eyes narrowed even more. What was this woman talking about with all these initials? His voice was edged by his growing impatience. "IV?"

"Intravenous tube, of course." Her own tone betrayed a thinning patience.

Matt didn't understand, but that was nothing new at this point; he didn't understand much of anything he'd heard since awakening. But as the wispy clouds receded from his mind, the suspicion grew stronger that he wasn't dead, after all. His lips tightening with determination to get clarification, he asked a point-blank question.

"Are you a nursing angel?"

"Nursing angel?" For a moment she appeared astonished. Then she laughed, producing a light, beguiling sound that affected Matt with the power of a lethal body blow. "Believe me, I'm neither a nurse nor an angel."

"Then I'm not dead . . . and in heaven?"

Her laughter vanished, to be replaced by a soft smile of compassion. "No, you are decidedly not dead."

Matt suffered conflicting feelings of wild elation and vague disappointment. Shaking his head in an attempt to dispel confusion, he sighed and inquired, "Then... where am I, and who are you?"

"As I said earlier, you are in a hospital recovery room," she answered in a warm tone—which sent chills skipping the length of his spine. "And I am Dr. Virginia Greyson... the surgeon who removed the bullet from your chest."

The chills along his spine intensified, but for an altogether different reason. His eyes flew wide, then narrowed again. "You are a doctor... a surgeon?"

Her smile could only be described as wry. "Yes. I am a doctor—" her incredulous tone mimicked his "—a surgeon." Her eyebrows lifted and her voice held a chiding lilt. "Now, don't tell me you have never seen a woman physician before today."

Matt was about to tell her exactly that, when his attention was drawn to the two women and one man who were suddenly surrounding the bed.

"Time to head 'em up and move 'em out, cowboy," the beefy, white-coated man drawled.

Wondering what the man was talking about, Matt shot a helpless look at his "angel," who claimed to be, of all things, a doctor.

"They are going to transfer you to another room," she explained.

Not seeing the point of the exercise, Matt frowned. "Why? What's wrong with this room?"

"Nothing," she answered, leveling a stern look at the others when they laughed. The laughter ceased abruptly, and she continued. "But this room is for postoperative patients needing constant care." Her features relaxed into a smile. "And I've just down-graded your condition from critical to serious."

"What does that mean?" Matt grumbled, feeling stupid and hating the sensation.

"It means you're being moved." She nodded at the others. "At once."

"I don't want..." he began in protest. She stifled his argument with one coaxing sentence.

"If you cooperate, I'll have someone get you something to eat as soon as you're settled."

Matt decided to cooperate—but not before gaining a concession from her. "Will you go with me?" He didn't see the grins twitching on the lips of the other three; his full attention was riveted on her reluctant smile, the indulgent note in her voice.

"Yes."

The activity that immediately ensued was bewildering for Matt. He was carefully shifted onto what looked like a narrow bed, but which the beefy man referred to as a gurney. Metal sides, much like those on a child's bed, were raised, and then Matt, gurney and the apparatus taped to his hand were rolled from the room and along a wide, brightly lighted corridor.

Every muscle in Matt's body clenched when the conveyance was rolled into what appeared to be a box-sized room with gliding doors. His stomach seemed to drop when the compartment slowly began a smooth descent.

Thoroughly rattled by the amazing, moving room, Matt was too fascinated by everything to do anything but glance around, trying to look at every aspect of his surroundings at once. Though the trip from one floor to the floor directly below was not far in actual distance, it encompassed a giant leap in time and space for Matt. By the time he was comfortably ensconced in the bed in his new room, he was utterly exhausted.

But Matt liked his new quarters and said as much to Virginia, the moment the other three had left the room.

"It's nice," he admitted.

"I know." Barely concealed amusement tinged her tone.

"Bright."

"Yes."

Catching the underlying hint of laughter in her voice, Matt shot a narrowed look at her. "Do you think this is funny, Doctor?" he asked softly.

She shook her head and bit her lip. "I'm sorry."

She didn't look sorry, but Matt let it pass. "You promised me some grub," he reminded her.

"And I always keep my promises." Pivoting, she headed for the door. "I'll be back in a minute with your...grub."

He opened his mouth to object to her leaving, but it was too late; she was gone. Disgruntled, Matt glanced around him, confused wonder filling his mind at the clean, cheerful look of the place. He had never personally been inside a hospital before, but had heard about them, and nothing he had heard compared in any way with what he was seeing. Of course, the most startling thing of all was that this obviously large, new building was located in a dying town in the foothills of the Anaconda Mountains in Montana.

Frowning at his thoughts, his gaze moved on, then settled on a small, windowed box placed upon a shelf on the wall. Now what in hell was that? he asked himself, exhaling a tired sigh. What could it be used for? He scraped his mind for a possible function for the box but came up blank.

Suddenly his head felt weighted, and his shoulder hurt. Absently rubbing the dressing over the wound in his chest, Matt rested his head on the soft pillow and continued to stare at the strange box.

Damn, he mused sleepily, this sure was a strange place. Closing his eyes, he decided he'd have to ask his "lady doctor" about two dozen questions when she returned with his food. But in a smaller number of seconds Matt was sound asleep.

He was out like a light.

The food tray in her hands, Virginia stood beside the bed staring at her sleeping patient. As rugged-looking as he was, the stranger appeared helpless, vulnerable in slumber. His impossibly long eyelashes brushed the shadowed hollows of his eyes, relieving the hard lines of his cheekbones and clenched, chiseled jaw. The pallor of illness was visible beneath the taut sun-darkened skin.

A tender smile crept across her lips as Virginia absently set aside the tray. The stranger was a tough-looking customer, and at the moment none too clean, and yet there was something about him that had touched her in an odd, inexplicable way. She didn't know him, but that didn't matter. From the instant she had first stared into his crystal-blue eyes, she had wanted him to live with every particle of her being, and with a sense of desperation that went way beyond anything she had ever felt for any other patient.

And now he was out, deep within the reaches of natural sleep, but he *was* going to survive the damage inflicted by the bullet wound in his chest.

The sense of relief Virginia experienced left her feeling drained and exhausted. She didn't understand any of the emotions she was feeling, and was too tired to examine them. For the moment it was enough to know that he would live, thanks to her skill as a surgeon—and perhaps to her fervent, if secret, prayers.

It was only then that Virginia realized that deep inside herself she'd been praying harder than ever before in her life. The realization startled her, for she was not as a rule what anyone would think of as a religious person.

Virginia shook her head, her smile tilting derisively. Praying...her? Incredible. Wasn't she the one, she chided herself, who had always believed it presumptuous to appeal to God in times of trouble—that is, if one believed in God to begin with?

Yep, that was she, Virginia acknowledged.

Yet, didn't she also know—from firsthand experience—of patients who had managed to defy reality by sudden cures? There was always the possibility of the unforeseen happening or—for want of another, logical explanation—the occasional miracle.

Now, bone weary, Virginia shrugged. When it came to the bottom line, who knew the answers? While it was true that there was no concrete proof to substantiate the existence of a Creator, in absolute truth, there existed no concrete proof against Him, either.

Wow! She really was tired! Virginia thought, dragging her gaze from the stranger's arresting face. When she started ruminating about the metaphysical, it was time to give the mind and body rest, she decided. She turned and strode from the room.

Less than five minutes were required for Virginia to divest herself of the unattractive operating-room greens she was still wearing, and pull on the dress she had slipped into for dinner.... Had it really only been last evening?

Shrugging into her coat, she headed for the double plate glass exit doors. She almost made it.

"Dr. Greyson, wait a minute!"

The call came from the front desk receptionist an instant after Virginia strode by. The woman had appeared swamped by questions from a group of holiday visitors, asking for room numbers and directions.

Smothering a sigh and raising her eyebrows, Virginia turned to face the other woman. "Yes?"

The receptionist nervously wet her lips at the note of impatience in Virginia's tone, but said bravely, "About the man who came in through Emergency last night..."

"Yes?" Virginia's tone now held a decided chill. "What about him?"

"I, umm..." The receptionist moistened her lips again. "I have no admittance forms on him."

Damn regulations, red tape and paperwork, Virginia railed inwardly. Tired to the point of barely managing to remain erect, she kept her temper by reminding herself that the receptionist was only doing her job. From somewhere she even found a smile for the hapless woman.

"I know." She shrugged. "He hasn't been conscious long enough for me to get the information from him." Her smile grew wry. "Are you getting flack?"

The woman returned the smile. "Of course."

Dumb question, Doctor, Virginia told herself, exhaling a sigh. You had better get home and get some sleep soon, she mused on, before the brain completely atrophies.

"Would you like me to send someone else for the information, after the patient wakes up?"

The receptionist's voice jarred Virginia out of her own meandering thoughts. "No," she said with a definite emphasis. "I'll be back later this afternoon. I'll get it for you then." Her mouth curved into a conspiratorial smile. "Do you think you can hold off Admissions until then?"

"I'll confuse them with overworked vagueness." The woman contrived a little-girl-helpless, wide-eyed look, which drew a burst of laughter from Virginia.

Still chuckling to herself, Virginia pushed against the plate glass door. As a blast of cold air hit her in the face, a parting call rang in her ears.

"Merry Christmas, Doctor."

Responding in kind, she stepped outside into the full bite of a frosty winter morning. After depositing upward of fourteen inches of snow on the ground, the storm had moved on. The sunlight reflecting off the mantle of white was a glaring assault on the eyes.

Squinting, Virginia burrowed into her coat and strode toward the hospital parking lot, confident that someone would have moved her car there from where she'd left it in the parking bay at the Emergency entrance. Her confidence wasn't misplaced; she found her car, cleared of snow, in the first slot marked Reserved for Doctors.

"Merry Christmas, Doctor," called the elderly gentleman stationed in the parking lot toll booth, as she waited for the gate to be lifted.

The greeting revolved inside Virginia's head, stirring the memory of her promise to have Christmas supper at the home of Richard's parents. Reminded of the commitment she had made, she groaned aloud.

Richard was to pick her up at her apartment at six that evening. On the other hand, *she* had moments ago promised to return to the hospital later that afternoon.

What to do?

Virginia worried the question like a dog with a bone during the short but tricky drive to her apartment complex. Should she call Richard and ask him to pick her up at the hospital? Or excuse herself from the date, citing business before pleasure?

But which was business, and which was pleasure?

The taunting query plagued her while she rode the elevator to her floor and trudged along the corridor to her apartment door. As she unlocked the door, a vision, unbidden and unwelcome, rose in her mind of the stranger lying alone and vulnerable in a hospital bed. At the same time, an echo of the proprietary note in Richard's voice at dinner—was it only last night?—replayed in her memory.

Dropping her coat and handbag onto the nearest chair, Virginia began undressing as she walked to her bedroom. Her shoulders were slumped from weariness, her eyes felt gritty and her mind had gone numb. She needed sleep—in her professional opinion, about twelve hours of sleep. A glance at her bedside clock told her it was 10:00 a.m.; she'd have to make do with less than five hours of slumber.

Virginia had long since learned to accept things as they were, rather than as she wished they would be. With a shrug, she picked up her phone receiver.

The first call she made was to her answering service, requesting a wake-up call for four. The second call wasn't nearly as simple. Richard was not happy about her canceling their date. He was inclined to argue. She was inclined to hang up on him.

Virginia fought down the inclination, but she hastened the conversation to its inevitable end, simply by refusing to allow Richard to prevail.

"I'm sorry, Richard," she said with more sincerity than she was feeling. "But if you'll remember, I've always told you that my patients come first...and I mean Christmas or any other day."

He objected.

She said a polite goodbye.

Minutes later Virginia was as dead to the world in sleep as the stranger who was her patient.

Three

God!

Matt stared in stunned amazement at the blond woman walking toward his bed. He had experienced a number of baffling events since awaking an hour ago, but the appearance of this woman was the most puzzling and interesting of all.

Without doubt she was the same woman whom he had earlier believed to be an angel. The woman had introduced herself to him as Virginia Greyson, a doctor and surgeon. And yet her appearance both baffled and shocked him.

Her hair was loose, attractively tousled by the wind. Her enticing lips were painted crimson, and looked slick and shiny in the glare of the bright overhead ceiling light. Gold hoops were fastened to her earlobes. A glittery bronze shaded her eyelids.

In comparison to the decent women of his acquaintance, who were all paint-free, she looked like a wanton. His nostrils quivered; damned if he couldn't smell her scent clear across the room. Wanton looking or not, she was the most beautiful female he had ever seen . . . the cleanest, too.

Feeling his body tighten in response to her, Matt lowered his eyes to her body—and experienced an even greater shock.

When he had first seen her after awakening from surgery, her hair was pulled back off her pale face, and she was dressed in what had appeared to be a wrinkled, shapeless green sack.

Now the sacklike covering was gone; its replacement caused a delightfully painful reaction in every particle of Matt's suddenly taut body.

She was dressed in a two-piece red thing—a short coat worn over a snow-white blouse. The bright red color of the coat lent a rosy glow to her cheeks. It was the bottom of the two-piece thing that rattled Matt. It was a skirt—of course, he knew that. But what shocked him was that the scarlet skirt barely covered her knees.

Matt scored a scandalized, appreciative glance down her shapely calves and neatly trim ankles, eyes widening as his gaze came to rest on her black shoes, which had narrow heels he judged to be at least three inches high.

Speculation gleamed from the bright blue eyes he raised to hers. In contrast, her doe-soft brown eyes were dark with question.

"Is something troubling you?" she asked in a musically soft voice that sang an alluring siren song all the way down his spine.

"There's a whole hell of a lot of things troubling me," Matt replied in a dry drawl, not mentioning that her nearness was suddenly the most troubling of all.

"Well, perhaps I can help clear up some of those things for you," she offered, smiling as she drew a chair next to the bed and settled her trim bottom on it.

You could clear up the most urgent of them by climbing into this bed with me, Matt thought. Aloud, he responded with a terse, "Maybe."

She was quiet for a moment, waiting, then arched her brows in that attractive way that did funny things to Matt's equilibrium. "Well?"

Distracted, he simply stared at her. "Well, what?"

She laughed on a sigh. "Not very forthcoming, are you?" She didn't wait for him to respond, continuing, "The nurse told me you're progressing surprisingly well, and that you were out of bed for a while after you awoke."

"Yeah," he muttered, "on your orders."

Virginia had to smile at the disgruntled note in his voice. "That's correct. I did leave instructions for the staff to get you on your feet. How did it go?"

"They didn't tell you?" His smile chided her.

"Yes, of course," she chided back. "Now I want to hear how you thought it went."

He shrugged, but admitted, "I felt a little wobbly, a little weak. I didn't like the feeling."

"Nobody does," she said, intuitively positive that he'd hate it more than most. Her brows inched up again. "How are you feeling now?"

"Hungry."

She appeared startled by his growled response. "But I was told that you had been served a meal!"

Deep in his throat Matt made a rude noise. "Maybe the folks around here call a swallow of broth, weak tea and a spoonful of some squishy, jellylike stuff a meal, but I sure as hell don't," he snapped.

"But a soft diet is necessary following surgery," she explained.

"Why?"

"Because of the anesthetic." Her smile attempted to soothe; his expression told her that it didn't work. She moved her shoulders in a half shrug. "Some patients experience nausea and even vomiting from it."

"I didn't," he said pointedly. His smile was designed to induce, if not actual fear, than at least trepidation in its receiver. Its feral quality had always worked for him before—it still did. Matt had to admit that the lady doctor had courage. He also had to admire the way she faced his teeth-bared smile without flinching.

"What would you like?' she asked, rising from the chair in one fluid move that intensified the chills still tingling at the base of his spine.

You, Matt thought, yearning to appease a deeper hunger. "Something I can sink my teeth into," he answered, searching out the softest, most vulnerable morsels of her body with a narrowed, raking glance.

The way her eyelashes flickered gave evidence that his silent message had been received. "I . . . ah—" she took a step back "—I'll see what I can do."

His low growl of satisfied laughter trailed after her as she hurried from the room.

Well . . . damn!

Virginia stood in the corridor beside the wall next to the stranger's room. She felt breathless and was trembling with an inner excitement. What was it about this man that affected her so? she wondered in amazement, staring in disbelief at the trembling of her fingers.

He was just another male patient among many and with his lank hair and dark bristled jaw a rather scruffy-looking one, at that.

Unlike many of her female acquaintances, Virginia had never felt an appreciation for a masculine five o'clock shadow. She preferred a man clean-shaven, shampooed and redolent of soap.

Nevertheless, this particular man had merely to look at her with his lids narrowed over those incredible blue eyes, and she had the distinct sense of something vital collapsing inside her. And the reaction she'd just experienced from his smile didn't bear thinking about.

Of course, while standing there, gulping in deep breaths, Virginia was powerless to think of anything else but the startling effects of his smile.

"Lost, Doctor?"

Virginia started at the question asked by a nurse she hadn't even seen approaching her. "Er, no." Virginia shook her head, contemplating the possibility of becoming "lost" to a stranger's uncanny attraction. "I was thinking."

"A problem with your patient?" The young woman indicated the stranger's room with a nod of her head.

"Actually, yes," Virginia said, her smile wry. "Not medical," she explained. "He's hungry."

The nurse frowned. "But he was served a late lunch a little while ago."

"He claims the meal left a lot to be desired."

"The first meal after surgery always does." The nurse laughed. "But the dinner trays will be served in less than a half hour."

Virginia glanced at her watch, then at the doorway to his room. She didn't relish the idea of telling him there'd be another half hour until dinner. "I'm afraid he's not going to be happy about the delay," she said with a sigh.

"We've got a fruit cake at the station," the nurse said. "I can give you a slice of it and a cup of coffee for him," she offered generously.

"Well, what are we standing here for?" Virginia said, flicking her hand in the direction of the nurses' station. "Let's get it."

Virginia reentered the stranger's room a few minutes later, a steaming cup of coffee in one hand and a small paper plate bearing a thick slice of fruit cake in the other.

"That's a meal?"

Suppressing an urge to dump the hot coffee over his straggly hair only by reminding herself of his weakened, postop condition, Virginia maintained her cool by gritting her teeth. "No, this is not a meal," she told him, grinding out the words, "but it will suffice until the dinner trays are served."

Virginia was expecting him to growl. Contrarily, his lips twitched with a secret inner amusement. But the twitch turned into a grimace when he tried to sit up unassisted. The curse he muttered was unprintable, if inventive.

Virginia wasn't shocked by the expletive; she had heard them all, or at least most of them. Patients, male and female, had a tendency to curse while under sedation.

"Lie still," she ordered, setting the cup and plate on the tray attached to the bed. "I'll raise the bed." Finding the control, she pressed the Up button, then found herself staring, fascinated by the amazed expression that filled his face and eyes as the head end of the bed slowly rose.

"Damn!" he exclaimed, grasping the mattress. "What kind of contraption is this thing?"

Thoroughly confused by his reaction, Virginia glanced from him to the bed, then back to him. "I don't understand," she murmured. "It's a common hospital bed."

He glared at her, blue eyes flashing angry, suspicious sparks. "There ain't a damn thing common about it."

"You've never seen an automatic hospital bed?" Virginia asked skeptically.

"I've never seen a whole helluva lot of the things I've been seeing in this place," he retorted. Releasing his grip on the mattress, he squirmed into a more comfortable position and reached for the piece of fruit cake.

"Like what—for instance?" Virginia asked, frowning as she looked around at the familiar, ordinary room.

He finished chewing the large bite of cake he'd taken into his mouth, and swallowed a gulp of coffee before answering. "Like that—for instance." He flicked his hand to indicate the TV mounted on a shelf on the wall. "What in Sam Hill is that thing, anyway?"

"The television?" Virginia frowned.

"Is that what it's called?" He peered warily at the set. "What does it do?"

Virginia's frown gave way to tolerant acceptance. "Are you having fun?"

Now he frowned. "What do you mean?"

"You're putting me on, right?"

"Putting you on?" he repeated, his frown deepening into a fierce scowl. "Putting you on what?"

"Playing head games," she said grittily. "Pulling my leg."

His scowl lifted at her last remark, to be replaced by an expression of utter confusion. "Why would I yank at your leg?" he demanded with such sincerity that Virginia was forced to believe him.

"You honestly don't know what a television is?" Her voice was soft, her tone one of awe. "What it does?"

His voice held an edge of panic. "Lady, I don't know what any of the things in this room are—or what it is they're supposed to do."

"Good grief!" Virginia stared at him in wonder. "You really were in the mountains a long time, weren't you?"

"Yeah," he agreed, but still looked skeptical. "But—"

"Never mind," she interrupted him. "Eat your cake, and drink your coffee before it gets cold. I'll do my best to answer all your questions after you've finished."

Her mind boggling at the task she'd set for herself, she returned to the chair beside his bed. As she settled onto the hard seat, her gaze fell on the clipboard lying atop the bedside cabinet. She sighed softly.

"Something wrong?" he demanded, eyes narrowing again.

"No, not wrong," she replied, picking up the clipboard. "I promised to fill out these forms and get them down to Admissions this afternoon."

"What forms?" he asked around the cup he was raising to his lips. "What are they for?"

"Admission forms," she told him. "And they're for the information on you that the hospital requires. They really should have been filled out before you were admitted."

His lips curled. "Paperwork."

Virginia smiled at the derision in his voice. "Exactly," she said in agreement. "Policy, regulations...and all that." She rolled her eyes. "But, since there is no escaping it, we may as well get it over with." She lowered her eyes to the first line on the form. "Name?" she asked, looking up at him with more curiosity than she cared to admit to.

"Matthew Hawk."

Virginia liked his name; somehow it fitted him. "Middle initial?"

His lips twitched in an intriguing way. "M," he answered with a rigidly straight face.

She was forced to smile. "Is there something odd or unusual about your middle name?"

The intriguing twitch melted into a grin. "My mother was a devout woman, read the Bible every day." He raised his brows promptingly. "Can you guess?"

Virginia didn't have to guess, she knew. "Mark?"

"'Fraid so," he drawled. "Ain't it pitiful?"

Virginia's spontaneous burst of laughter eased the tension that was coiling along her nerves. "Oh, I don't know," she observed. "I think it's rather nice."

"Only another woman would," he observed in a dryasdust tone, finishing off his coffee. He shot a glance at the door, then at her. "When did you say supper would be coming?"

"Soon," she assured him, smiling and shaking her head. "Meanwhile, can we get on with this?" She tapped her pen against the form.

He shrugged. "Shoot."

She complied. "Home address?"

"Fort Worth."

Virginia's head jerked up. "Texas?"

"There's another one?"

"But—" she began, frowning.

"Can we get this over with?" he cut her off irritably.

"Certainly," she snapped. "Occupation?"

"United States marshal," he responded at once.

"Really!" Virginia stared at him in stark astonishment. The way his lips twitched sent a thrill of warning through her.

"Now, Doctor," he drawled. "Would I put you on?"

"Incredible," she retaliated. "I had no idea the United States Government hired idiot savants as marshals."

Matthew Hawk didn't appear insulted; he looked interested. "What's an idiot savant?"

Virginia literally threw her hands into the air. "Oh, never mind!" she cried. "Date of birth?"

"June 13, 1854."

That does it! Virginia decided with disgust. She would not be the brunt of his humor any longer. Raising her head, she glared, prepared to verbally blast away at him. The angry words dried on her lips as she met his clear-eyed stare.

He wasn't kidding!

The realization raised the hair on Virginia's scalp, and she had the weird sensation of having been plunked down smack in the middle of the Twilight Zone.

Telling herself to get a grip on herself, Virginia cleared her tight throat. "You do mean 1954 ... don't you?" she asked in a please-tell-me-I'm-right whisper.

"1954?" He exploded with laughter. "1954! Lady, are you loco?"

Virginia had an eerie feeling that she didn't want to think about, let alone investigate. He was joking, she assured herself, either joking or stark, staring mad. That was it, he was....

A chill shuddered through her body as her memory flashed scenes into her mind, scenes of the way he was dressed when she'd first seen him, scenes of the way he had been reacting to his surroundings since regaining consciousness. She saw again his cold eyes, the frightening expression on his face when he'd demanded to know what she had done with his pistol.

Staring now into those eyes, which were staring back at her in question, she began to tremble.

But it wasn't possible! He had the appearance and the physiological structure of a man in his mid-thirties. Unless he had discovered the fabled fountain of youth, he couldn't possibly be...

"Are you telling me you are over a hundred years old?" she demanded irately.

His jaw dropped. "Over a hundred?" he repeated, eyeing her warily. "Lady, you're not loco, you're plain crazy!"

Virginia shook her head very slowly. "I don't understand any of this."

"Well, don't think you're riding point alone," he growled. "I haven't understood anything about this place ever since I woke up."

Virginia's heart was beating so rapidly that she could barely breathe, never mind speak. "O-okay," she said, between gasping breaths. "Let's see if we can clear up the mystery. Suppose we start at the beginning. I want you to tell me exactly how your accident happened."

"Accident, hell!" he exclaimed. "I was bushwhacked."

"In the middle of the street?" she cried.

"No!" Now he shook his head. "I was on the path, heading for the church at the top of the hill."

"What hill?" Virginia envisioned the street where the police had found him—the level street. "Where?"

"Here." He waved his arm, as if to indicate not only the room but the entire area. "Right here in the Anaconda Mountains in Montana."

Virginia could feel her eyes growing wide. "You were shot in Montana?"

"No, I was shot in the chest," he retorted with dry humor. "But I was here in Montana at the time."

His humor sparked her temper. "You can make jokes if you like, Mr. Hawk, but I feel I must tell you that you are not anywhere near Montana. You are in a hospital in the town of Conifer, Pennsylvania."

The humor disappeared from his eyes, leaving them hard and shrewd looking. "You are crazy."

"No, I am not," Virginia snapped. "And—for your information, we are in the last decade of the twentieth century."

"And—don't tell me," he said in an infuriatingly soothing voice. "You're Annie Oakley?"

"Of course not!"

"Belle Starr?"

Virginia had reached the absolute end of her patience. "I've had enough of this!" she said, jumping to her feet and slamming the clipboard onto the cabinet. "What kind of games are you playing?"

"Games? Is that it? This is a game to you?" His eyes narrowed on her face, while his hand tugged at the covers. "I'm wounded, and you want to play games. I see, but no thank you, ma'am." As he spoke, he pushed aside the covers.

Thinking that now even the Twilight Zone had begun to tilt, she cautiously said, "No, I don't want to play games. And where do you think you're going?"

He grimaced with pain as he slid to the edge of the bed. "I am getting out of this madhouse," he said with determination.

"No!" Virginia cried, reaching out to stop him. "You're in no condition to leave!" Her hand brushed his arm, and she was startled by the sudden heat she felt on her fingertips. Her palm grew moist, her throat went dry. There was a definite lack of substance to her voice, and no authority whatever. "You'll reopen that wound."

"Too bad," he retorted, grunting as he thrust one leg from beneath the covers. The short hospital gown he was wearing revealed his leg from his bare foot to his long, lightly haired, tautly muscled thigh. "Dammit! Where's my pants?" he growled, glancing around. "And where are the rest of my things...my clothes and my gun?"

Distracted, confused, Virginia dragged her gaze from his naked thigh and her hands away from his arm to motion toward the dresser opposite the bed. "In there, I suppose." Blinking herself out of her bemusement, she argued, "But you can't leave now. You're not well!"

His lips curved again into that cold, feral smile. "Who's gonna stop me, lady?"

Who indeed? Virginia gave a brief thought to hospital security and even the police, but immediately dismissed the idea. Instead, she shivered...and backtracked. "Look, I'm sorry I upset you." She raised her hands in a placating gesture. "Please, Mr. Hawk, stay in bed. I'm positive we can work this through...somehow."

He hesitated, eyeing her warily. "I want my things." His voice was low, his tone adamant. "Will you bring them to me if I stay in bed?"

Considering it a small concession, she nodded. "Yes, if you insist on seeing them."

"I do." Moving slowly, teeth clenched against the jarring pain in his shoulder, he shifted toward the center of the bed, then hesitated once more. "There's something else."

Virginia stiffened, instantly on guard. "And that is?" she asked cautiously.

"I'm called Matt."

The pent-up breath she'd been unaware of holding eased from her constricted throat. Virginia hadn't known what form his request would take, but she had never expected him to ask her to use the diminutive of his given name. The sense of relief that washed through her left her feeling weak and produced a shaky smile. "All right . . . Matt."

"And I'll call you Ginnie."

Since she had never cared for that particular nickname, Virginia made a face. "I prefer Virginia." Her tone held a deliberate, I'm-in-charge-here, edge.

His grin left her in little doubt of who actually was in charge of the situation. "I prefer Ginnie." He waited, half in half out of the bed, for her reaction.

She shrugged. "Whatever."

Matt cocked one dark eyebrow. "Is that an okay?"

Virginia gave him a don't-push-your-luck stare. "Yes, Matt, that is . . ." Her voice trailed away as a nurse carrying a tray swung into the room.

"Sorry dinner is late," the nurse said in a cheerful voice. "But I don't think you'll be upset when you taste the special holiday meal you're getting." She slid the tray onto the narrow, tablelike attachment to the bed, then turned and smiled at Virginia. "Hi, Dr. Greyson."

"Hello, Marsha," Virginia said, returning the pleasant young nurse's greeting, while silently encouraging Matt's struggle to position himself closer to the food tray.

The nurse turned to leave, then paused at the doorway. "Oh, can I bring something for you, Doctor? Coffee, tea?"

Virginia was about to politely decline the offer when the aroma wafting from the tray caused a pang in her stomach, reminding her that she hadn't eaten since the previous evening. She had felt confident on leaving her apartment a short while ago that her business at the hospital—checking the progress of her patient and getting those dratted admittance forms completed— would take her less than an hour. After that her time would be her own, since she had canceled her engagement to join Richard and his parents for supper. She had even entertained the idea of returning home, fixing a light meal, making herself comfortable in front of the TV, and enjoying a ghostly Christmas movie.

So much for that plan, Virginia thought with a sigh. Besides, since she had as much as said she would pay the hospital costs, if necessary—and from the looks of things it would be—she might as well derive something from her generosity, even if it was only a meal.

"Yes, thank you," she finally replied. "I missed lunch, and I'd appreciate a dinner tray."

"Coming right up," Marsha called, swinging out of the room. She was back with the second tray moments after Virginia pulled the chair nearer to the bed.

Virginia sat, hands folded in her lap, until the nurse swept from the room once more. She watched in fascination as Matt studied the plastic-wrapped utensils next to his plate, and she ached somewhere deep inside when he looked at her in blank appeal. Feeling a rush of sympathy for him, she remained silent, but made a detailed production of tearing open the plastic and removing the knives, forks and spoons.

A crooked, self-deprecating smile tilting his lips, Matt followed her example—to the letter. When he had freed the utensils, he carefully loosened the napkin wrapped around them. Frowning at the white plastic cutlery, he laid the pieces aside, then proceeded to tuck the napkin under the material of the gown where it edged his throat.

Fully expecting him to tear into the food, Virginia was nonplussed when he didn't as much as touch the domed cover over the plate, but sat patiently, staring at her.

"Is there something wrong?" she asked, shifting her puzzled eyes from his tray to his face.

"No, ma'am."

"Then why aren't you eating?"

Matt looked affronted. "My mother taught me manners while I was still in britches." He inclined his head toward her tray. "I'm waiting for you to begin."

Under the circumstances, his display of simple, old-fashioned gallantry pierced Virginia to the core of her being. He was hurt and angry, and more than a little disoriented and confused. He was also very hungry. And yet this strange and strangely attractive man sat still and quiet, waiting for her to begin the meal.

The ache deep inside Virginia spread. Her sympathy crystallized into an overwhelming feeling of protectiveness. She didn't know this man, but in that instant she didn't care. Her mind was filled with questions about him, but they could wait. Thoroughly disarmed, but completely aware of what she was doing, she smiled and lifted the cover from her plate.

Four

Feeling better?" Virginia smiled and ran a casual glance over the two trays. The plates and side dishes were literally scraped clean of the contents, of which she had eaten less than half.

"Mmm." Matt nodded. Cradling his coffee cup in one broad hand, he relaxed against the pillow that supported his back. "This is good coffee." He took a sip and raised his dark brows into a teasing, nudging arch. His eyes gleamed at her over the rim of the cup.

"Would you like some more?" Virginia's low voice contained understanding laughter.

"Yes." He drained the cup and held it out in front of him. "Please."

She gave him a wry smile, but stood and walked from the room. Moments later, she returned with the half-full glass coffeepot from the nurses' lounge. "It's not good for you, you know," she informed him, re-filling both his and her own cup with the steaming dark brew.

"No?" His eyebrows went up again. "Why not?"

"The caffeine, of course." Her smile chiding, she leaned forward to add milk and sugar to the liquid in his cup. "It rattles the nerves."

"I don't have any nerves," Matt said. His nostrils flared slightly as he inhaled. "Smells good."

Straightening, Virginia smiled and fussed with the dishes on the tray. "The nurses make good coffee."

"I wasn't talking about the coffee," he said, grinning at her as he took a tentative sip. "Although it smells good, too."

Virginia felt a fluttering sensation glide along her spine. "What . . . were you referring to?" she had to ask, even though she instinctively knew the answer.

Matt's bright eyes grew dark and heavy-lidded, and glittered with a blatant, sensual glow. "You, and the perfume or whatever it is that you're wearing," he murmured. "I can smell you clear down to my gut." His voice became low, raspy. "Makes me think of dark nights and darker bedrooms. I like it...the smell, and the hot-cold feeling it gives me inside."

The fluttery sensation along Virginia's spine intensified, causing a hot-cold feeling inside her, too. Determined not to think of dark nights and darker bedrooms, yet trembling in a reaction that was out of all proportion to his compliment, she moved to sit on the chair beside the bed. A startled gasp broke from her throat when he reached out and curled his fingers around her wrist.

"You feel it too, don't you?" His voice was still lower, even more raspy than before.

"No!" Virginia exclaimed, emphasizing her denial with a sharp shake of her head. "I don't know what you mean." Feeling vaguely alarmed, yet strangely excited, she pulled against his hold on her. His fingers tightened, not painfully, but in an oddly secure and sensual way.

"Don't you?" Matt persisted, continuing to smile at her. Draining the cup with a couple of deep swallows, he set it beside hers on the tray. His fingertips brushed against the tender skin on the inside of her wrist, and his voice grew still deeper, soft with a knowing sexiness. "Come into this bed with me and I'll show you."

Her pulse began to hammer and her mouth went dry. The awareness of him as a male, a dangerously attractive male, drowned her normal common sense. The urge to acquiesce to his invitation, however, clashed with her natural reserve and helped to restore her equilibrium.

Chastising herself for her juvenile reaction to him, Virginia brought her senses under control by exerting sheer willpower and advising herself to grow up. She'd had similar invitations from other male patients, and had always laughingly rebuffed their overeager postoperative amorous advances.

Telling herself that this man was no different from the others, and that in actual fact he was a lot less clean looking than all her previous male patients, Virginia did manage to conjure up a faint smile.

"I'll pass, thank you," she said, tugging once more against his encircling fingers.

Matt frowned. "Is that a no?"

"It is." Virginia gave him a reproachful look. "You're in no condition to perform, at any rate. So—" she arched her eyebrows "—could I have my arm back . . . please?"

Though Matt stared at her indignantly, he did release his grip on her wrist. "What do you mean, I'm in no condition?" he demanded. "Come closer, and I'll—"

"Probably reopen your wound," Virginia interrupted, carefully stepping back out of harm's way. Her wrist tingled, but she won an inner battle against the urge to rub her fingers over the spot he had imprisoned and brazenly stroked.

"I won't reopen the damn wound," he said, dismissing the idea with a shrug. "Being wounded never interfered with my . . . ah . . . performance."

Virginia gaped at him. "You've been shot before?"

"Twice." Matt nodded in affirmation. "Once in the leg, once in the side."

"But that's incredible!" she gasped.

"Not too," he drawled. "I'm a lawman."

His terminology struck a discordant note in her mind. Lawman? The last time she had heard the expression was in a Western film she'd half-heartedly watched on TV. "Hmm, that explains everything."

"Sure." He grinned at her. "Besides, I'm feeling better all the time. The grub did the trick."

Grub. Virginia shook her head, but asked, "Then you enjoyed your meal?"

"That was the best Christmas dinner I've had since I left home."

Virginia was suddenly alert. "When was that?"

"When I was seventeen, the summer of seventy-one." A challenging smile bared his hard-looking teeth. "Eighteen and seventy-one."

His words, his phrasing, instilled a tremor inside Virginia. Because the tension between them had dissipated during the conversation they had engaged in while eating dinner, the sensation was even more shocking than before. She gave him an imploring look.

"Please, Matt, don't start that again." Virginia was too rattled to notice that she sounded more like a concerned woman than a detached professional.

"Start what?" Though his voice remained free of inflection, his eyes revealed renewed wariness.

"This silliness about dates!" she cried.

"It's not silliness to me," Matt retorted. "I know what year I was born. I know what year I left home. I also know when and where I was ambushed. I was shot last night, Christmas Eve, eighteen hundred and eighty-nine."

Since Virginia was a surgeon, not a psychiatrist, she wasn't certain how to proceed in handling his apparent delusion. Yet she felt that she must break though to him, if only because in every other respect, Matt appeared stable and well balanced. Acting intuitively, she turned and again headed for the door.

"Where are you going now?" he demanded.

"For proof," she answered without breaking stride. "I'll be back in a moment."

As Virginia had expected, there was a folded, much-read newspaper at the nurses' station. After receiving permission to borrow it, she clutched the paper in one hand like a weapon and marched back down the corridor and into Matt's room.

"There," she said forcefully, slapping the paper, front page up, onto the bed. "This is the special holiday edition of today's paper," she went on, tapping the headline with one slim finger. "Please note the date."

After subjecting her to a hard, narrow-eyed stare, Matt lowered his eyes to the paper. A shudder, visible and intense, shook his body. The face he raised was pale, the brilliant blue of his eyes was dulled by confusion. His voice, so confident moments ago, held an uncertain tremor.

"I don't understand."

"That makes two of us," Virginia replied. "Taking everything you said at face value, I have no idea where you got the idea that it was 1889, and that you were in the mountains of Montana when you were shot." Again she tapped her finger against the paper. "As you can see, this paper not only has the correct date but the location, as well. The police found you lying in the middle of the street, and you are now in a hospital in Conifer, Pennsylvania."

Matt didn't return his puzzled gaze to the paper, but continued to stare at her as he slowly shook his head. "Police...in the street...Pennsylvania?" he muttered in disjointed spurts.

"Yes." Though quiet, Virginia's tone was firm, unequivocal, straightforward.

His broad shoulders drooped an instant before he sagged back against the pillow. He was quiet for long seconds, as if trying to assimilate her assertions. When he looked at her again, his gaze was sharp. "You think

I'm crazy and need a head doctor," he said. "Don't you?"

"Not at all," Virginia denied, with what she hoped was reassuring promptness. "I believe your mind is probably suffering from shock due to the combination of your wound and exposure."

"But, you see, Doctor, I'm not confused about what happened or where and when it happened," Matt murmured. "The only things I'm confused about are the things that have happened since I woke up, clearheaded, a little while ago."

"But you do know it's Christmas Day?"

Matt shot her an impatient look. "Yes, I know it's Christmas Day. We just finished eating the holiday meal." His voice was strong and his features grew taut, vanquishing the expression of uncertainty and defeat. Sitting upright, he straightened his shoulders, as if infused with renewed purpose. "I also know that I was shot last night, Christmas Eve, nineteen hundred and eighty-nine." His lids narrowed over glittering eyes. "What I don't know is how I got from Montana to here . . . or why I'm not dead."

Virginia's sigh said volumes about her growing sense of frustration; the way she raked a hand through her hair underscored every line. For whatever reason, Matthew Hawk was certain he was from another place and century. And unless she could convince him to face reality, and soon, she knew she would be left with little option but to call upon the expertise of a psychiatrist.

Virginia generally held the field of psychiatry and her colleagues practicing in that field in the utmost esteem. At any other time, with any other patient, she would not hesitate in seeking their assistance. Yet now she felt justified in pausing to reflect.

She had noted the unvoiced trepidation in Matt, had correctly read his body language and facial expression when he'd asked her if she believed him to be crazy.

In Virginia's professional opinion, Matthew Hawk would react to the presence of a "head doctor" in exactly the same manner as he would react to a coiled rattlesnake.

So that left it up to her. Virginia concluded that, at least temporarily, she'd play it by ear. But how and where to begin? Staring into his wary eyes, she decided the gentle route would be lost on him. Matt was obviously tough, and in her opinion, equal to a mild form of shock therapy.

Testing her theory, she reached for the TV remote control and pressed the On button. As the screen flickered to life, the voices of a choir, raised in exultation, blared from the speakers. Virginia was both amazed and fascinated by Matt's response.

His eyes growing wide with unmistakable shock, grimacing with pain, Matt scrambled backward, as if attempting to escape danger by pushing himself through the headboard of the bed and the wall behind it. His breathing was harsh, irregular. The pulse at the base of his throat fluttered wildly.

"What in hell!" he exclaimed, staring at the screen with an expression of stark disbelief. "How did they get all those little people in that box?"

In other circumstances, his reaction might have been funny. But the fear visible beneath Matt's incredulity left little room for humor. The fear and amazement on his strong-featured visage were not a laughing matter.

Intuitively and intellectually, Virginia knew he wasn't faking. She was convinced that Matt's response was a genuine reflection of what he was feeling. Simultaneously, deep inside, she felt a growing suspicion that everything he had said about himself and his origin was the absolute truth. In the name of sanity she denied it—but she felt it.

"There are no little people inside that box," she replied with calming reassurance.

He flashed a confused look at her. "Then how—?" He broke off, returning his gaze to the TV set. "Then how can I see them? How does it work?"

Good question. Exactly how did it work? Virginia was flooded with a sense of inadequacy. Like most, her comprehension of the technology that had produced television was limited. She simply accepted it, along with all the other many wonders of modern science.

"I don't know how it works," she said, impatient with her own ignorance. "But that's not important now. The thing is—Are you listening to me?" she asked, in a tone sharpened to draw his fascinated attention away from the special Christmas production that was being presented on one of the network channels.

"Huh?" Matt turned his head and blinked at her. "Oh, yeah, you said you don't know how it works." He shrugged. "That's okay. I don't know how the steam engine automobiles work, either. But I know they do, because I saw one." He raised his eyebrows. "You ever see one?"

"An automobile?" Virginia asked, fighting against an inner sense of unreality.

Looking at her in a way that indicated *she* was acting strangely, Matt nodded in response.

"I own one."

He frowned. "I can't figure out why in hell anyone'd want one. They make one helluva noise."

An eerie chill permeated Virginia's body as she realized again that Matt wasn't acting or playing some sort of sick game with her. He was dead serious. Perhaps, she mused, feeling a crushing sense of failure, she'd be better advised to seek psychiatric counsel, after all.

"Why are you looking at me like that?" he asked, startling her from her reverie. "What are you cooking up inside that beautiful head of yours?"

At that, the first thought to flash into Virginia's head was: did he really think she was beautiful? The thought was immediately followed by another, this time a self-ridiculing condemnation. What difference did it make whether or not he thought her attractive? Her appearance had little to do with the matter.

Still, Virginia experienced a secret thrill of pleasure from his left-handed compliment.

Mentally shaking off the unusual effect she was feeling, she instilled a stern note into her tone. "I'm not cooking up anything, and if I'm looking at you in any strange way, it's simply because I'm trying to decide exactly what it is you're hoping to gain by claiming to have been shot in Montana in 1889."

Matt bolted upright to glare at her. "If I'm trying to gain anything," he said in a deadly hard voice, "it's to make some sense out of this whole crazy business."

Virginia felt the raw anger from his glittering eyes all the way to her toes. Suddenly fearful that she just might be dealing with a raving lunatic, she held out her hands in a pacifying gesture. "All right, calm down," she said, careful to keep her own voice soft and soothing.

He actually sneered at her. "I'm not an infant to be spoon-fed pap and crooned to," he snarled, his eyes shooting fiery sparks at her. "Get me my things."

The abrupt demand threw her off balance. "What?" she asked, and immediately added, "Why?"

"My own things," he answered, in an unpleasant tone. "Because I want them . . . now."

Virginia didn't even contemplate refusing him. In fact, she didn't pause as much as a moment to reflect. Jumping up, she moved to the built-in closet and dresser drawers in the wall opposite the bed. She found his clothes hanging in the closet, his hat and boots on the floor beneath them, and his personal effects in a large plastic bag in the top dresser drawer. Not stopping to examine them, she scooped them into her arms. The bag was bulky and heavy. Frowning at it, she turned and dumped the lot onto the bed.

"Thank you." Sarcasm laced Matt's voice.

"You're welcome." Virginia matched his tone. "Would you care to tell me what you intend to do with them?"

"Yeah, I'll tell you," he retorted. "I intend to get dressed and get the hell out of here."

"But you can't!" she cried in protest.

"No?" His lips thinned, twisting into a sardonic smile. "Watch me."

She didn't doubt him for an instant. Virginia instinctively knew that if he said he would do something, he would do it...come hell, high water or an anxious physician. She also knew she had to stop him.

"Your wound," she said, infusing authority into her voice. "You're in no condition to leave the hospital."

Matt flexed his shoulder, grimaced, then shrugged. "I've traveled with worse." His eyes became hooded as he raked her face and figure with a bright, hot glance. "Too bad. You're one tempting lady, and I'd've liked nothing more than getting to know you better...a whole lot better." He sighed, but shrugged again. "But I will be damned if I'll hang around and listen to you call me a liar."

"I didn't!" Virginia exclaimed in heated denial, while silently denying an inner melting sensation caused by the sensuous heat that was blazing from his eyes.

"You did!" Matt growled. "Oh, maybe you didn't say it outright, but I'm not stupid. I don't need the words spelled out for me." He laughed harshly. "You believe I'm either a bald-faced liar or crazy as a critter set loose in the loco weed...don't you?"

She shook her head. "No, as I said earlier, I think you're still suffering the effects of—" She was interrupted by the slicing motion of his hand.

"I'm not in shock," he said. "I told you, I'm clearheaded and thinking straight." He reached for the clothes she'd dropped in a heap at the foot of the bed. "And I'm getting out of here."

"To go where?" Her question was deliberate, designed to stop him. It succeeded.

His hand hovering above the pile of clothes, Matt raised consternation-filled eyes to hers. "You were telling the truth? This place really is in Pennsylvania?" His voice held a note of uncertainty that pierced directly to her heart.

Virginia sighed. She was no longer sure which one of them was unbalanced. What she was suddenly sure of was that she couldn't bear that uncertain note in his voice. The entire situation was insane, and yet she felt an overwhelming desire to reassure him, if only to bring back the angry fire into his eyes and the ring of confidence into his voice.

"I'm no more a liar than you are, Matt," she said softly. The expression darkening his eyes tore at her.

"How did this happen, Ginnie?"

At the pleading note, Virginia raised her hands, then let them drop in a helpless gesture. "How can I answer you?" she cried. "I'm as much in the dark as you are!" He opened his mouth to speak, but she silenced him with a quick shake of her head. "I'm not suggesting that you're a liar or confused or anything else." She smiled through a deep sigh. "Look, why don't you start at the beginning and tell me exactly what happened, and we'll work on it from there?" Her smile tilted coaxingly. "Okay?"

His sigh echoed hers. "Okay."

His story took the better part of two hours. In a tired-sounding tone devoid of inflection, Matt began his recitation with the day of his birth—in June 1854.

Biting her tongue to keep herself from interrupting him, Virginia listened in astonishment as Matt painted a sketchy but vibrant verbal picture of life and the frequently hazardous conditions of growing up in the freewheeling West of the latter half of the nineteenth century.

Against her will and common sense, Virginia found herself caught up in his story. She was there with him, feeling his sense of despair and helplessness as he witnessed his father's death beneath the slashing hooves of a maddened horse. She wept inwardly with the seven-year-old boy he had been, trying to take some of the burden from the shoulders of his overworked mother as she grew old too soon laboring to eke out a living from a small, unproductive ranch. And Virginia was by his side, wilting in the intense glare of the summer sunlight, as Matt the man, his taut, harshly set features concealing the agony clawing at his insides, stood beside a hole in the ground, watching his mother being lowered into her final resting place.

In expressionless tones stark with inner pain, Matt unwittingly revealed the frustration he still suffered from knowing that the relative ease he had been able to provide for his mother from the time he'd become a man—at the advanced age of fifteen—until her death before he'd reached his majority, was too little and had come too late.

She waited in breathless silence when he paused, absently reaching for her untouched coffee. Watching the tendons flex in his strong throat as he tossed back the now tepid liquid, a funny little ache stirred deep inside her. When he resumed speaking, she had the uncanny sensation of actually feeling the dry harshness that shadowed his voice.

Unwilling, yet powerless against the strength of his narrative, Virginia rode beside Matt, wearing the badge of a United States marshal, in the pursuit of outlaws. She knew he was nearing the end of his story when he told of his month-long assignment, trailing a particularly vicious killer into the Anaconda Mountains of Montana.

So vivid was his description of that Christmas Eve, so poignant the despair and revulsion he had felt at the necessity of killing the outlaw, that Virginia, too, shivered in the crisp night air and felt his sickness of spirit deep within her own body and soul.

Matt stared bleakly into her face. "I was...am...so damn tired of living on the trail and watching my back. I had decided to quit, to get as far away as I could from law enforcement. It's kinda funny how it turned out." An ironic smile curved his thin masculine lips. "I was on my way to the church at the crest of the hill for Christmas Eve services. Goin' begging to the Lord for a fresh start on a decent life." A new shudder rippled the length of his rangy body. "Instead, I got a bullet in the chest." His eyebrows lifted into a sardonic arch. "The Lord's callin' card, maybe?"

His last remark shattered the remaining shreds of Virginia's objectivity. "No!" she cried out in protest. "You're here, you're alive!"

"Yeah, I'm here and I'm alive," Matt retorted. "But why am I here, in this place?" He didn't allow her time to respond, but continued. "And dammit! Why am I alive? I was dying. I knew I was dying. So why ain't I dead?"

Virginia recalled him asking the same question earlier. On hearing it repeated, she had a flashing memory of the first time she had seen him, lying still and sprawled in the street, staring sightlessly into the falling snow. She recalled, too, the one policeman's reply to his partner's comment about the victim's eyes.

"Well, of course his eyes are cold. He's dead."

She herself had believed him to be dead, Virginia remembered, suddenly trembling...and she was a physician!

What did it mean? It didn't make sense. None of it made sense. Here he was, very much alive, and yet slightly out of sync...out of time. Virginia would have bet her professional reputation that Matt wasn't acting, lying or deluded.

That left ... what?

Virginia was afraid to contemplate the answer to the riddle of Matthew Hawk. She was also afraid that she knew the—unacceptable—answer.

Out of time.

The phrase revolved in Virginia's head as she stared into the eyes of the man, the stranger, seated taut and expectant on the bed.

Was it possible? she asked herself, while the certainty of that possibility welled up inside her. But how? she demanded in silent desperation.

Even as her mind groped for explanations, she heard again Matt's whispered words. An answer?

"Goin' begging to the Lord for a fresh start on a decent life."

Virginia swallowed against a sudden tightness in her throat. Had the Lord granted alms of life to the beggar?

The rational, logical part of Virginia's brain immediately rejected the hypothesis. Things of that nature
simply didn't happen, couldn't happen...not in the
waning years of the twentieth century.

But couldn't they...didn't they? a tiny inner voice
demanded. Think, remember. Earlier she herself had
recalled instances she'd witnessed, and others she'd
heard about from colleagues, of the unexplainable and
seemingly miraculous recovery of terminally ill patients.

But time travel? Virginia was slowly shaking her
head in repudiation of the very idea, the very way-out
idea, when the sound of Matt's rough, impatient voice
jolted her from her introspection.

"Well, say something, dammit!"

"What do you want me to say?" she cried.

"You heard my story." His body was quivering
from tension. "Do you believe me?"

"Yes, I believe you."

He exhaled harshly, as if he'd been holding his
breath for a long time. "You said that maybe we could
figure out what happened. Do you have any ideas?"

Without pausing to consider, Virginia blurted aloud
the speculation that had lodged in her mind. "Do you
think it's possible that you were transposed from then
to here through some sort of time warp?"

Five

What in hell is a time warp?''

"No. Forget it." Virginia shook her head, as if to literally shake herself back into the world of reality. "Just forget it."

"Forget it?" Matt repeated in a baffled tone. "How can I forget it? I don't know what *it* is."

Virginia gave one final shake of her head. "It was too farfetched, a ridiculous idea."

"What was a ridiculous idea?" Matt raked a hand through his hair in frustration, then grimaced at the sheen of oil slicking his palm.

Virginia shifted her gaze from his shiny palm to his hair. It was long, lank and shaggy—looking exactly like one would expect on a man who had spent over a month on the trail of a criminal...and quite like every photograph she had ever seen of men in the old West of the late eighteen hundreds, over a century ago.

Ridiculous? Virginia repeated the conclusion to herself. Yes, of course it was, but, then again... She jumped, startled, when Matt reached across the bed to grasp her hand. His long fingers quivered from the tension still gripping his body.

The weathered, sun-bronzed skin on his face was drawn tight over his strained features. "Dammit, Ginnie, tell me what you're thinking!" His voice held a raw, pleading note that went straight to her heart. "I'm lost—help me."

His cry was the deciding factor for Virginia. Irrational, illogical, inconceivable as her idea definitely was, it was still the only one that made sense.

"Okay." Virginia surrendered with a sigh. "I'll try to explain." She gave him a warning look. "I'm afraid it is going to sound more than a little crazy to you."

Matt shrugged. "Right now everything seems more than a little crazy to me." His lips tilted in a crooked smile, easing the tension that had formed grooves around his mouth. Visibly relaxing, he loosened his grip on her hand, then, instead of releasing her, he entwined his fingers with hers. "Even a crazy explanation is better than no explanation."

The warmth of the fingers curled around hers caused a shivery feeling inside Virginia and interfered with her breathing process. Though only their hands were touching, she experienced the uncanny sensation of feeling him with every particle of her body.

Talk about ridiculous, she thought, staring at the sprinkling of dark hairs on the backs of his fingers. At that moment, she would swear she could feel the texture of every one of those wispy hairs.

"Ginnie?" The puzzlement in Matt's tone shattered her reverie.

"What?" Virginia's head snapped up. "Oh, yes, my idea." She paused to draw a calming breath.

"Is something wrong?"

"No," she denied, shaking her head and collecting her wits. "Ah...I was thinking." Along dangerous lines, she thought.

Matt's fingers tightened for an instant. Leaning toward her, he brought his face close to hers...his mouth close to hers. His voice grew low, seductive. "About me?"

His breath swept over her lips. From eyes wide with surprise, Virginia could see every masculine nuance of his chiseled features, every individual stalk of dark stubble on his squared jawline. And she could smell the slightly musky male scent of him. His unique fragrance went straight to her head, permeating her senses, defusing her defenses.

"Ginnie." Breathing her name, Matt advanced, moving his mouth nearer, ever closer to hers.

"Matt." His name little more than a yearning whisper, Virginia parted her lips to receive his.

The touch of his mouth was at first tentative, then, on a low growl, tenacious. She felt the gentle but commanding rake of his teeth along her lower lip an instant before his mouth forced her lips farther apart. The gentle savagery of his mouth against hers stole both her breath and her sense of propriety. Sighing, she returned his kiss with equal fervor. His response was immediate and devastating. His tongue swept into her mouth, deepening the kiss into an erotic play evocative of a more complete possession.

Virginia felt his kiss, the penetration of his tongue to the very depths of her femininity. With mindless abandon she clung to his mouth, drinking sensuous sustenance from him as greedily as he devoured the sweetness of her. When he withdrew, releasing her mouth with obvious reluctance, her breathing was as harsh and labored as his own.

"Why...why did you do that?"

Smiling, Matt raised his hand, drawing her fingers to his lips. "Because I wanted to," he said with simple directness. He kissed her fingertips, sending shards of sizzling awareness throughout her body. "I've had a hankering to kiss you ever since I opened my eyes and saw you this morning, there in that room you called the ICU unit."

"Really?" Virginia felt like an idiot for voicing the question, but she didn't care. In fact, at that moment she didn't care much about anything. On the fringes of her mind, she knew she was acting, reacting, in an uncharacteristic manner, but she didn't care about that, either. What she did care about was the sensations he was creating inside her by stroking his tongue over her fingers.

"Yes," Matt murmured, curling his tongue around one finger and drawing it into his mouth. "And since this morning, the hankering's grown into something fierce." Though his voice was raw, muffled, she heard every word.

"It...it has? In what way?" Virginia knew, yet a need that had been buried and suppressed, demanded she hear his answer.

His laughter was low, dark, exciting. "In every way imaginable," he replied, staring candidly into her wide eyes. "I've been itchin' to tear your beautiful, shocking clothes off and pull you into this bed. I want to feel you, warm and soft, beneath me."

Virginia was already soft, from deep inside to the surface of her skin, soft and warm and . . . astonished at herself. She also noted his use of the word *shocking*. Dragging her gaze from his hooded, sexy eyes, she glanced down at her clothing. She agreed with part of his remark. The suit and blouse were beautiful, but . . .

"Shocking?" She frowned and raised her eyes to his. "What's shocking about my clothes?"

Matt's gaze drifted to her legs, and lingered appreciatively on the exposed expanse of nylon-clad calves and ankles. "Not that I'm complaining, you understand," he said, a slow smile curving his lips as he returned his gaze to hers. "But you've only got half a skirt, and I never have seen heels that high on a lady's shoes."

The term "lady" was a tip-off. Comprehension dawned in Virginia's mind, clearing the fog of sensuality. It also underscored her belief in his credibility.

"You really are from the nineteenth century," she said in a tone of sheer awe. "Aren't you?"

Her question had an immediate, deflating effect on him. All the fire and passion visibly drained from him, leaving him looking exhausted and bereft. He heaved a deep sigh. "Yes, I am from the nineteenth century," Matt replied in weary tones that tore at her heart. "I swear that everything I've told you is true, Ginnie."

"I never doubted that you believed what you were telling me, Matt," Virginia said softly. "But I—" She broke off, startled by his sudden violent curse and movement.

"Dammit, Ginnie, I am not crazy!" he exploded. "Look at this!" Letting go her hand, he reached for his belongings at the foot of the bed. "I want you to look at this stuff, examine all of it, and then tell me I'm crazy."

Virginia was hurting for him, hurting so badly that her throat ached and felt raw and tight. "Matt, I never said that I thought you were—" But again he cut her off, this time with a sweeping gesture and a rough command.

"Look at it, damn you."

An odd sensation coiling in the pit of her stomach, Virginia moved to obey. With a sense of disbelief and amazement she identified the sensation as fear. Matt looked so fierce, sounded so angry that he actually frightened her. Speechless with incredulity, she reached out for an article of clothing. She was obviously too slow to satisfy him.

"Look at this," he ordered, scooping a heavy, thigh-length, dark-colored coat from the pile. "And these," he continued, holding aloft a jacket and pants, both obviously made from the same black, rough-textured material.

Having registered the fact that morning that his attire appeared to be from an earlier epoch, Virginia was nodding in mute agreement when he growled a low curse.

"Dammit, that was my best shirt." Clutched in his big hands was a white shirt with a small hole and a large bloodstain on the right front breast panel. "It's ruined," he muttered, reaching again for the coat and jacket. "And so are both of these." Shaking his head in disgust, he dipped his hand into the pocket of the coat and withdrew a mangled-looking small pouch and a packet of papers. "The wet soaked through to my makin's," he murmured in a mournful tone.

"Makin's?" Virginia repeated.

Matt gave her an impatient glare. "My tobacco and papers," he said. "They're soggy, useless. Wouldn't you know it? Just when I needed a smoke, too."

Virginia's response was automatic. "You shouldn't smoke, anyway. It's unhealthy."

Matt stared at her for what seemed to stretch into a very long time. "First coffee, now tobacco." His lip curled. "Next you'll be telling me sex ain't healthy."

No, she wouldn't be telling him that. Virginia kept her response to herself. To avoid a reply, she returned her attention to his belongings. The boots and hat were well-worn, similar to yet different from their modern counterparts. "What's in the bag?" she asked, raising her eyes to his.

"Not much." Matt shrugged. "I travel light." Grabbing the bag, he pulled it to him, then proceeded to empty the contents onto the bed. There was underwear—a pair of long johns—all in one piece. There was a pair of thick, off-white socks. Next he produced an official-looking badge, with the words United States Marshal carved around the rim. After the badge, he withdrew a large silver pocket watch, the lid of which was beautifully chased with the outline of a locomotive. The final article was the largest and deadliest looking of the lot. In her opinion, a gun and holster were not a pretty sight.

"Ugly things," she said, giving way to the shiver of revulsion moving through her.

Matt frowned as he shifted his gaze from her to the holster, then back to her. "Ugly?" he echoed indignantly. "I'll have you know that this here is a hand-tooled scabbard, made to my specifications for this Colt Peacemaker." As he spoke, he drew the long-barreled pistol from the leather holster, and held it out for her inspection.

Virginia recoiled as if he had offered her a ticking bomb. "I don't like guns!" she exclaimed.

Matt made a wry face, but shoved the revolver back into the holster. "The gun won't hurt you, you know," he drawled. "It can't do a damn thing all on its lonesome."

"I've heard that argument," she snapped. "I still don't like guns." She suppressed another shiver. "I'd appreciate it if you'd put it back in the bag."

"In a minute," Matt promised, smiling faintly. "The scabbard carries a few things other than artillery." Turning it over, he began poking at the inside of the broad belt.

Watching him, Virginia frowned and asked a question. "Why did you call it a scabbard?"

The glance he shot at her said reams about what he thought of her intelligence. "Because that's what it is."

Controlling her irritation, she retorted, "I know that casings for rifles are called scabbards, but I've never heard the term in reference to a pistol."

"That so?" he drawled. "Strange, but where I come from it's called a scabbard."

"Not a holster?" she persisted.

Matt shrugged. "By some, maybe. Mostly by greenhorns."

Studying him while he continued to poke his fingers along the inside of the belt, Virginia decided that Matthew Hawk could prove to be a living, breathing history lesson on the life and times of the old West. Intrigued by the possibilities he presented, she wasn't paying much attention to the objects he removed one by one from small slits in the belt. She jumped when he let out a muffled whoop of satisfaction.

"Aha! There you go," he announced, dropping a handful of shiny gold coins onto the bed in front of her. "I'd be obliged if you'd take some of those and buy me a new shirt."

Some of those? Systematically counting the coins, Virginia was jolted once again by shock. The gold coins appeared newly minted...all bore the date 1889. At face value, their total amounted to $275. She couldn't begin to as much as guess at the value of the coins to a numismatist.

"Where did you get these?" she asked without thinking, glancing at him in surprise.

"Well, I sure as hell didn't steal them," he shot back at her. "I was paid right before I left Texas, tracking that longrider."

"I didn't think that you stole them," Virginia protested. "And what is a longrider?"

"An outlaw," Matt said. "And what did you think, if not that I'd stolen the money?"

Virginia felt as though she had been plunged back into far-out land. "I didn't mean anything," she said in soothing tones. "I was just so surprised. Do you have any idea what these coins are probably worth?"

"Sure, $275," he replied, frowning.

"No." Virginia shook her head vigorously. "They were worth that in 1889," she said. "I couldn't begin to evaluate their worth to a numismatist on today's market."

"A new what?"

"Nu-mis-ma-tist," she enunciated. "An expert who collects rare coins."

"Well, fancy that," he murmured, smiling in a secret, contemplative way. "You really think these couple little coins are valuable, then?"

"Yes." Confused, and suspicious of his enigmatic smile and attitude, Virginia narrowed her eyes and demanded, "What are you thinking?"

"Right now, this minute?"

"Yes."

"I'm thinking that I've gotta go." He moved restlessly and glanced around the room. "If you would just point me in the right direction, I'd be much obliged." Favoring his shoulder, he began shifting to the edge of the bed.

"Wait!" Virginia flung out an arm to stop him. She missed. He slid off the bed and stood up...to a height she judged to be at least six foot three. "You don't have to get up. I'll call the nurse for the bedpan."

"No, thank you, ma'am." Matt gave a short, decisive shake of his shaggy head. "The nurse brought that pan in this morning." He shuddered. "I'm not going through that embarrassment again. Tell me where it's located. I'll go out."

Out? Virginia's mind went blank. When she realized what he meant, she went pink. "For heaven's sake, you don't have to go outside!" Jumping up, she strode to the closed bathroom door. Pushing the door open, she indicated the room beyond with a flick of her hand. "It's in here."

He gave her a dry look. "I should've known. Even back in my time I'd heard about them."

Virginia's eyebrows flew up. "Really."

"Yes, really," he drawled, moving toward her.

The regulation hospital gown he was wearing did little to conceal his long-muscled, rangy body. Feeling her avid interest in the width of his shoulders, the narrowness of his waist and hips and the powerful length of his legs unprofessional, Virginia drew her fascinated eyes away from him. Her gaze flew back to his when he laughed softly.

"Now don't tell me the sight of a nearly naked man embarrasses you," he murmured as he stopped beside her. "And you a doctor, ma'am."

What Virginia could have told him was that the sight of a man, nearly or fully naked, hadn't embarrassed her since her second year of medical school. It was only the sight of *his* nearly naked body that had this effect on her. Of course, she didn't tell him any of it. She didn't say a word. Managing to look superior she gave another, impatient flick of her hand toward the bathroom.

She followed him inside. He turned to scowl at her. She offered him a sweet smile. "Wouldn't you like the accommodations explained?"

"Make it quick."

She did. "I'll be right outside the door if you should need me," Virginia said, retreating.

Fighting persistent images of his too-attractive body, while denying the pull of attraction she was feeling for him, she stood outside the bathroom door, alternately hoping he'd need her help and praying that he wouldn't. She heard the loud rush of water from the flush, then a less forceful flow from the sink tap. She started when he suddenly pulled open the door.

"What is all this stuff?" Matt asked, frowning at the plastic case he was holding.

"This is a very up-to-the-minute hospital," Virginia informed him in smug tones. "That case contains the basic necessities a patient might need."

"Yeah?" He arched his dark brows. "But, like I said, what is it all...what's it for?"

With amused forbearance, Virginia named the articles and described their use as he removed them one by one from the case. "Toothbrush—to clean the teeth," she said when he extracted the plastic-handled brush.

"I knew that," he retorted. He pulled out one of several small tubes. "This?"

"Toothpaste." She grinned. "To clean the teeth."

Matt looked impressed. "I always used salt." He withdrew another tube.

"Bath and shower gel."

"Like soap?"

"Yes." She fought a smile.

"What's a shower?"

The smile won. "I'll show you in a minute. Next?"

Yet another tube was withdrawn. "This is the last of these little things."

"Shampoo." Virginia bit her tongue to keep herself from adding that he really had use for that particular product. "For cleaning the hair."

"What's wrong with soap?"

She shrugged. "Too harsh."

Matt snorted derisively. "And this?" He held up a small pump spray plastic bottle.

"Deodorant." She nearly choked on the word. Before he had a chance to ask, she explained. "After removing the cap, you hold it like this and depress the button," she said, demonstrating as she spoke.

"Perfume?" he said indignantly.

"No, it's antiperspirant." Virginia frowned. "Well, there is some scent added."

"Uh-huh." He returned the bottle to the case.

Virginia hid a smile. "I'm sure you recognize the pocket comb and brush. Any other questions?"

"What's a shower?"

She burst out laughing. "You're like a dog with a bone! Okay, pay attention." Walking past him, she drew back the curtains to reveal the tub and shower. Bending over, she turned the water taps. "You adjust the cold and hot flow until the water is the temperature you prefer. Then you flip this switch—" again she demonstrated "—and there's your shower," she finished as the water sprayed forth.

"Thank you," Matt said politely. "Now get out."

"What?" Virginia stood erect and turned to stare at him. "Why?"

"Because I'm going to test the shower."

"Oh, no you're not!"

"Oh, yes, I am." His smile dared her to argue further. "Would you like to test it with me?"

"No, thanks," Virginia retorted, thinking that men obviously never change. "You'll soak the dressing on your wound."

His grin widened. "That's okay. My doctor can apply a fresh dressing when I'm through."

After years of confrontations with patients, Virginia had learned when to stand and fight and when to cut her losses and withdraw; since Matt was yanking at the gown with supreme unconcern, she chose prudence and withdrew.

Matt was beneath the shower spray for a good half hour, during which Virginia put away his clothing and other belongings, got a clean gown and a robe out of the drawer for him, and then paced the small room. In the back of her mind, she registered the tinny announcement over the PA that it was eight o'clock and visiting hours were now over.

The wait was worth the agitation. When he walked out of the bathroom, Matt looked like a different man. His chiseled, angular face was shaved smooth. His towel-dried but still damp hair was gleaming clean. And he looked rawly masculine but almost presentable in the tightly belted cotton robe.

"You do a good job of work, lady," he said, raising his hand to his right upper chest. "That's the neatest I've ever been sewed up. The others are kinda rough and jagged."

Virginia winced at the description. "I'll be the judge of that. Come over to the bed and sit down, and I'll have a look at it," she instructed in her most professional tone.

"Yes, ma'am," he said smartly, padding bare-footed to the rumpled bed.

Giving him a wry look, Virginia carefully moved aside the gown and robe. On viewing the wound, she was forced to agree with him. Her skill was apparent, and the wound was healing nicely. "I work neat," she drawled, reaching into the bedside cabinet drawer for a packaged sterile dressing.

"And I feel like a new man." Perched on the edge of the bed, Matt grinned at her as she tugged the robe into place over the fresh bandage she'd applied to his wound.

His innocuous remark triggered a memory that ricocheted through Virginia's mind. "Matt," she said in a small voice. "If the idea I had about your situation is correct, you *are* a new man . . . in a new place."

"What do you mean?" he asked, losing his grin to a frown. "Are you talking about that time warp thing?"

"Yes." Virginia sighed.

His eyes were cool, his voice was steady. "I think it's time you explained it to me."

"Yes, I think it is." Sliding onto the chair pulled up to the bed next to him, she began, "I don't know much about it, myself, but I'll explain as best I can." She paused to sort through her thoughts. He gave her a verbal nudge.

"Shoot, time's a'wastin'."

"Well, as I understand it, there have been some stories and reports of people who, caught in some manner of a warp or crack in time, have been transposed from one period of time to another, both back-ward and forward. It's commonly called time travel.

These stories and reports are all undocumented and unsubstantiated, of course."

"Do you believe that this time travel is possible?" Matt's bright, shrewd eyes pierced hers.

"No." Virginia drew a deep breath before qualifying, "At least I didn't until today."

Matt was quiet for several minutes. When he did finally speak, his voice held a faraway, thoughtful softness. "Do you think that's what happened to me... that I was somehow picked up there and dropped here?"

"I don't know, Matt," she answered honestly. "But I can't think of any other explanation."

"Hmm," Matt murmured, nodding. Then, suddenly rigid, he asked, "Do you think it could happen again? I mean, that I'd be swept up here and dumped down there again?"

Virginia was developing a pounding headache. Massaging her throbbing temples, she gave him a helpless look. "I don't know. As I told you, I really know very little about it. Up until today I assumed the theory of time travel was pure fiction."

Matt looked as helpless as she felt. He nodded in agreement, but said, "Yet here I am."

"Yes." The single word held a wealth of emotion.

There ensued a long period of silence, during which both were sunk in their own thoughts. Matt shattered the quiet with a soft, anguished cry.

"What am I gonna do, Ginnie? I can't go back over a hundred years... can I?"

"No." Answering him was difficult, but even more difficult was the terrible thought that suddenly occurred to her. The image of a woman, perhaps with her children around her, rose to torment Virginia. "Matt!" she exclaimed. "Are you...were you... married?"

He gave a quick but reassuring shake of his head. "Never stayed in one place long enough," he replied. He paused, frowning, then said slowly, "It's funny, but a woman, a wife, was one of the reasons why I was going to church last night—" He caught himself, then corrected, "that night."

"I don't understand." Virginia felt a stabbing twinge that she wasn't inclined to examine. "Do you mean you were going to the church to meet a woman?"

"No. I didn't know any of the women in that town." Matt shrugged. "But I had decided to quit, turn in my badge." Unconsciously he mixed his tenses. "I'm so tired of it...the hunt and the kill when nothing else works but killing. I was thinking that there had to be a better way to keep the peace, and a better way to live."

The brilliant blue of his eyes dimmed and grew opaque. "I was thinking of a decent life...starting with a horse ranch, nothing big, just a small outfit to begin." His smile was weary, and sympathy welled up within her. "I suppose what I was planning to do was ask the Boss for a second chance, with a place of my own, a child of my own, a woman of my own." He gave a short snort of laughter that held little humor. "Instead, I find myself in a strange place, in a strange time, with a box with little people in it, and a woman who believes I'm loco."

Near tears, Virginia impulsively reached out to grasp his hand. "Matt, no, I don't believe that, truly

I don't." Until then she had only a vague idea of how disoriented and displaced he must be feeling. The enormity of the sensation he had to be experiencing hit her like an actual blow. "You're not alone, Matt. I'm here."

His eyes cleared and he smiled at her. "I appreciate that, but it's not being alone that bothers me. I've been alone a long time. I'm used to it." Moving his head slowly, he glanced around the room. His fingers tightened around hers when his gaze settled on the television set, still animated and blaring away on its shelf. "I don't understand half of what I've seen and heard since I woke up. I can't go back, and I don't know my way around your time and place." He turned to her, his expression stark. "Ginnie, when I leave your hospital, I'll have nowhere to go."

While he was still speaking, Virginia thought of a solution to his dilemma. She blurted it out before she had a chance to change her mind. "You're wrong, Matt. You do have someplace to go to when you leave here."

"Where?"

Virginia was already regretting her impetuousness. Nevertheless, she replied in a steady voice. "You can stay at my place."

Six

Now that she had him, what in the world was she going to do with him?

Wondering if she had lost her mind, Virginia shut the door and slumped back against it. Resting her head on the smooth panel, she stared at the man standing in the center of the living room.

What had possessed her to offer him the haven of her home? He was a stranger, not only to her but to everyone in the community. Virginia had regretted her impulsive invitation moments after making it, but she hadn't had the heart to retract it. He had looked so lost, so vulnerable.

While she was questioning herself and studying him, Matt was taking slow, comprehensive stock of her apartment. Her reaction to seeing him there, seeming to dwarf her private space, was as unnerving and thought-provoking as his appeared to be...if his expression was anything to go by.

Thirty-odd hours had passed since Virginia had made the impulsive offer to Matt. During that period, every one of her waking hours had been crammed full with seventy minutes' worth of things to do. Through some innate wizardry she hadn't realized she possessed, she had managed to complete every one of those things...except provide him with "the makin's" he had asked her to pick up.

Matt's reaction to her offer was immediate and grateful—and followed at once by a demand to know when he could leave the hospital. He had seen his wound when she'd redressed it, and knew that it was well along in the healing process. Arguing that he was feeling, in his words, "Strong enough to lick my weight in wildcats," he pressed her to release him.

Since her professional opinion coincided with his argument, Virginia made a bargain with him, telling him she would allow him to leave if he behaved himself for one more day. Matt gave her his word, and she was left with little more but to follow through on her promise.

In retrospect, and under the circumstances, she decided that the sooner he was safely installed in her apartment, out of sight of curious eyes and questions, the better.

Virginia had encountered the first of those eyes and questions as she was leaving the hospital around nine o'clock Christmas night. Carrying the admission form, which she and Matt had reworked together—in her opinion a creative piece of fiction, indeed—she had run into Jeff Klein, the young patrolman who had been at the scene of Matt's advent into the twentieth century.

"I'm on my way in to see your patient," Jeff said. "I stopped by before I went off duty this morning, but the nurse told me he was asleep." His smile was tired. "I need some information for my report. I hope he's awake."

"Sorry, Jeff. I just left his room, and he's out for the night." Virginia uttered the untruth with a silent prayer for forgiveness. "Perhaps I can help you." She displayed the admission form. "I have all the pertinent information on him, but I must warn you that there isn't much."

"I'll say," he muttered, scanning the form. Producing a notebook from his inside pocket, Jeff jotted down the information. "Did he tell you anything about what happened?" he asked hopefully, returning the notebook to his pocket.

Because she and Matt had rehearsed the account to be given, Virginia was prepared to answer. "Yes, but again, there really isn't all that much."

"Some cops have all the luck." Jeff sighed. "Okay, I'm listening. Fire when ready."

Virginia registered in passing the realization that men seemed to have a penchant for identifying with guns. Matt had said "Shoot," and now Jeff said, "Fire when ready." She couldn't help but wonder if there were some psychological, quintessentially masculine reason for the association. Maybe she'd discuss the idea with the hospital's resident psychiatrist. Then again, maybe she wouldn't. The staff psychiatrist was a gun collector.

Shrugging off the odd thought, Virginia launched into the story that she and Matt had concocted.

"Well, from the sketchy information he's given me, I gather that Matthew Hawk is a drifter. Not a vagrant, a drifter," she hastened to clarify. "As you've seen from the admission form, he is originally from Texas...Fort Worth, and was drifting through Conifer when the accident occurred."

"Accident?" Jeff queried, raising his eyebrows into a skeptical arch.

"Hmm." Virginia nodded. "Mr. Hawk insists the shooting must have been accidental, since he doesn't know anybody in the area, and hasn't been here long enough to have made any enemies. He suggests that perhaps the accident was caused by a youngster, secretly fooling around with some adult's rifle." She held her breath when she finished, positive that Jeff would reject the theory. To her astonishment, he didn't.

"Possible," he said thoughtfully. "Around here, more than possible." He sighed once more. "Was there any identification on him that I missed when I searched him? Driver's license? Social security number? Anything?"

"No, nothing. All we have is what he told me." Virginia swallowed and plunged. "Really, Jeff, I believe you can write this one off as an accident, caused by person or persons unknown, and forget it."

"He was wearing a gun, Doctor!" Jeff exclaimed. "And I've been kicking myself all day for not taking it off of him when I had the opportunity."

"Oh, come on, Jeff!" Virginia forced an easy-sounding laugh. "Every other male in this community owns a gun and either wears it or carries it at some time or other."

"Yeah." Jeff nodded. "Even so, I'm going to run a record check on him through Fort Worth and Washington, just in case he's wanted somewhere."

Lots of luck, Virginia thought wryly. Aloud, she agreed that the precaution was wise. "Let me know what you learn about him," she added, with more interest than Jeff could imagine, or than her casual tone implied.

Virginia slept badly Christmas night. She had arrived home to find three messages from Richard on her machine. She listened to his injured-sounding voice, then without a qualm erased the tape, reset the machine, and dropped into bed. Yet sleep eluded her. Her tired mind whirled with disjointed fragments of the day, the first day of her holiday break.

What a Christmas present! Virginia thought, muffling an incipient burst of hysterical laughter. Time travel! It was simply too much—too weird, too outlandish. Who would believe it? She was finding it nearly impossible to believe herself.

But Matt was real . . . Lord, was he real! His searing kiss attested to that. Virginia's lips still burned, her senses still vibrated in response to his sensuous brand of reality.

But time travel?

Impossible. There had to be another explanation. The concept of time travel was the stuff of fiction.

But . . . how to explain Matt's genuine bafflement?

Matt.

When Virginia finally did fall asleep, it was with unanswered questions teasing her mind and the taste of a nineteenth-century man on her lips.

It was early when she awoke, startled from slumber by a dream in which she was flying through space and time, with the sound of Richard's voice calling to her to come back.

Getting up and dragging her tired body from the rumpled bed, Virginia caught a glimpse of herself in the mirror and decided she looked like the leftovers from the holiday meal....

And now, watching in silence as Matt examined his new surroundings, Virginia smiled and ran an appreciative, self-congratulatory glance over his new attire.

Armed with her credit card and the measurements she had taken from his clothing, she had left the apartment early yesterday morning to do battle with the throng of shoppers, eager to take advantage of the traditional day after Christmas sales. The chore had been exhausting, but the results were definitely worth the effort expended.

The articles of clothing she had selected for him were identical to the winter apparel that the majority of male residents generally wore: jeans, plaid flannel shirts and an outer jacket, in this case a ski parka instead of the more usually seen hunting jacket. She had purchased socks and packages of underwear for him, as well. So Matt should have looked much the same as every other man in town.

He didn't, and the difference couldn't solely be attributed to the Western hat pulled down low on his forehead or the scuffed boots sticking out of the bottom of his jeans. No, the difference between Matt and every other man Virginia had ever met involved much more than mere appearance, even though the way he looked played a large part in it.

The soft material of the shirt delineated the width of his shoulders and the breadth of his flatly muscled chest. The jeans appeared to have been made expressly for his long, rangy body, riding low on his hips and smooth over his narrow, tight buttocks.

In summation, on Matt the clothes were not an affectation or a fashion statement, but a reflection of a man of his time. The clothes fitted—in more ways than one. The only item missing was his gun belt, and that was hidden inside one of the store bags he had set on the floor next to his booted feet.

Observing him as he absently removed the hat and parka, Virginia concluded that Matt looked even less like the more formally dressed businessmen in the community—a hundred years less like them.

An image of one such businessman came to mind. Frowning in concentration, she attempted to draw a comparison between Matt and Richard Quinter. It was an exercise in futility, because there *was* no comparison. Though Richard was without question handsome, urbane and up-to-the-minute in his choice of attire, he paled into insignificance beside the more simply clothed, magnificent presence of Matthew Hawk.

Odd. She had always considered Richard to be the epitome of maleness.... Virginia's thoughts scattered as Matt chose that moment to turn to look at her.

"It's all...all..." His voice faded, as if he couldn't find words to describe his feelings.

"All a bit much to take in?"

"Yeah." Matt gave her a wry smile. "I think I might still be in shock from the ride."

Recalling his expression at his first sight of her car when they left the hospital, Virginia laughed. "You didn't appear in the least shocked," she said. "As a matter of fact, I would have sworn you enjoyed the ride immensely."

Matt's eyes gleamed with amusement. "As a matter of fact, I did. It sure as hell beats freezing your butt on the back of a horse." He laughed. "Come to that, it's a damn sight faster and more comfortable, too."

The enticing sound of his laughter curled around her heart. In an effort to combat the growing familiarity of the warmth that was spreading through her, Virginia pulled her expression into stern lines of disapproval. "You swear a lot," she said in a cool, chastising tone. "Don't you?"

"Sure." Matt's teeth flashed dazzling white in a teasing grin, giving silent testimony to one of the three twentieth-century conveniences he had quickly become addicted to; Matt loved the taste of toothpaste. He also loved standing under the shower and staring at the television screen. "Must've picked it up from the company I keep."

"*Used* to keep," Virginia said, reminding him that he was no longer in the old West.

"Yeah." He sighed. "Even with all I've seen in the last couple days, it's still hard to believe."

"I know."

"I suppose it's a lot for you to handle, too," he said, smiling faintly.

"Yes."

His smile widened into a grin and he nodded toward a spot behind her. "I can't help but wonder. Are you propping it up, or is it supporting you?"

"What?"

"The door." He arched an eyebrow. "Are you too tired to move, or are you hanging there by the door to make a quick break, if I jump in the wrong direction?"

Reminded in turn of the kiss they'd shared Christmas night, Virginia was suddenly infused with a different kind of warmth. Both startled and made wary by the blatant sensuality of that warmth and her own responsive heat, she had avoided close contact with him since then. How she was going to manage now, with him installed in her apartment, was the question she had yet to answer.

"No, of course not," she denied, straightening as she stepped briskly into the room. "I was giving you time to get accustomed to the apartment."

His eyes glittered, silently calling her a liar. "Is this the whole of it?" he asked, glancing around the room.

"No," Virginia replied, slipping out of her coat as she walked by him. "This is the living room. Let me hang your jacket and hat in the closet, then follow me. I'll give you the grand tour of the place and show you your room."

The apartment was spacious, and equivalent in size to an average house. Virginia didn't rent the place, she owned it. It contained a kitchen with a tiny dining area attached, the living room, three bedrooms, the smallest of which she had made into a den, a central bath and a half bath connected to the largest bedroom. It was tastefully furnished, yet homey and comfortable—the kind of place where a woman or man could relax after a rough day on the job.

Matt was noticeably impressed by the size of the place and its furnishings and appliances. "This is all yours?" he asked as they returned to the living room. "And you live here alone?"

"Yes." Virginia laughed. "This is my home."

His brows shot up in surprise. "It's yours?" Matt asked with undisguised incredulity. "You own it?"

"It's mine." Virginia felt a thrill of justifiable pleasure and pride in what she considered the fruits of her skill and dedication to her chosen profession. "I own it."

Matt responded true to form. "Damn," he murmured, skimming his gaze around the room. "The house I grew up in wasn't half this big or half again this pretty." He returned his gaze to her, stunning her with a blaze of undiluted admiration. "You are one impressive lady, Doctor."

Delighted by the compliment, warmed all over by the heat from his eyes, Virginia was reduced to a flustered stammer. "Why, tha-thank you! I...I'm..." Not sure herself what she wanted to say, she averted her gaze from his gleaming eyes and changed the topic. "Ah...I suppose we ought to get you settled," she improvised, catching sight of the bags containing his things. "If you'll grab those bags, I'll—" The sudden sharp ring of the phone interrupted her.

The trilling ring had an astonishing effect on Matt. His head snapped up and his eyes, narrowed and alert, searched out the source of potential danger. Although there had been a phone on the cabinet beside his bed, and Virginia had explained the functioning of the instrument to him, it had not rung once during Matt's short stay in the hospital.

The instrument might be something of a marvel, but not to the extent of transmitting a call from the Montana of the 1890's, Virginia thought, commiserating with his reaction.

"It's only the phone, Matt," she said in a calming voice. "If you'll excuse me, I'll be with you in a—"

"Go ahead," he interrupted her, his lips curving into a self-mocking smile. "I can find my way."

Tossing him a quick smile in return, Virginia took off at a run for the kitchen phone.

Gathering up the store bags, Matt headed for the room she had told him would be his. His long strides faltered at the breathless sound of Virginia's voice as he passed the archway into the kitchen.

"Oh, hello, Richard."

Irritation flickered inside Matt as he continued into the short hallway leading to the bedrooms.

Richard? he thought, swinging shut the door to his room with more force than necessary. Who in hell was Richard?

There was no way he could know the answer to his question. He knew practically nothing about Virginia in general, and nothing at all about her personal life in particular. A scowl drew Matt's dark brows together at the realization that he in fact knew nothing about much of anything in this strange new world in which he found himself.

Crossing the room, he dropped the bags onto the bed, then stood looking around at his temporary new home. Even though Virginia had apologized for what she called the room's sparse utilitarian furnishings—

a plain single bed, dresser and nightstand—Matt liked the room. It was by far cleaner, brighter and better furnished than any other room he'd ever had. In truth, he liked the entire apartment, with all its intriguing gadgets and appliances yet to be investigated. But most of all Matt liked Virginia, and was looking forward to investigating her, even more than the gadgets and appliances.

Virginia.

Merely thinking her name set Matt's blood on fire and caused a sweet, painful tightness in his body. A vision of her as she'd entered his room on Christmas morning filled his mind. Tall, slender, breathtaking, with her shining blond hair flowing around her shoulders and her beautiful legs exposed to his hungry gaze. At his very first sight of her, he had thought he'd died and she was an angel, but when she'd come to his room later with her face painted and her legs revealed, he had equated her with the loose women of his acquaintance...not an angel at all, but a wanton.

Matt had never been slow to learn. And through that amazing box she called a television, he quickly realized that her attire, her enhanced coloring and her overall appearance were the style of the day. Virginia looked like every other female he saw on the TV, only better...a whole helluva lot better.

From the very beginning, she had created an ache inside him that gnawed and fiercely tortured his body. More than anything he'd ever wanted before in his life, Matt wanted Virginia. But all he had received so far was a large dose of frustration.

Because she had kept her distance from him since Christmas night, he had only kissed her that one time, yet one kiss had fanned the flames of his desire into an insatiable appetite for more of the same. A taste of Virginia was not nearly enough for Matt; he craved, nay ached, to devour her like a sumptuous banquet, beginning with her luscious mouth and ending...

Matt shuddered and longed for a cigarette. Damn, how he wished Virginia had bought him the makin's he had asked her to get.

Virginia. To Matt she was richer, headier than the tobacco from the state that bore her name. And his need for her was infinitely stronger than his desire for a smoke.

In an attempt to suppress both, Matt absently stowed his few belongings in the deep dresser drawers. Although the bags were quickly emptied, he wasn't very successful in controlling either one of his clamoring desires.

The chore finished, Matt sat down on the bed and tried to ignore his appetites by contemplating his present situation.

How had he gotten here? he wondered, glancing around at the room that existed, in effect, over a hundred years after his own time. Even though Virginia had explained the theory of time travel to him, Matt was having difficulty in believing, let alone accepting her explanation. And yet everything he had seen since regaining consciousness confirmed that he was definitely not in the same time frame he'd been in when he was shot.

Recalling the events of that Christmas Eve, Matt frowned in concentration.

He had been tired, filled with despair, a sickness growing inside him against the kind of life he was living. He had been on his way to church. Seeking what? Solace? Redemption? Or simply to beg God for another chance, for a decent life, for a...

Matt's thoughts fragmented, then regrouped to focus on his thinking process during those final moments before he had lost consciousness. He had been thinking that there would be no second chance, no decent life, no *woman* of his own, and then...and then he had cried out, invoking God's name, silently screaming that he could not die. And when he had regained consciousness, he had opened his eyes and seen...

Virginia!

Stunned by the implication, Matt's mind went blank for an instant. When it cranked up again, it spun off thoughts almost faster than he could assimilate them.

Feeling the lifeblood draining from him after he'd been shot, Matt had felt, known he was going to die. And yet here he was, not dead but very much alive. Had he been granted another chance by calling on the name of God? Had some spiritual hand plucked him up in the hills of Montana and set him down again in the mountains of Pennsylvania, right in the path of this one particular woman?

Matt shook his head like a greenhorn whose senses had been rattled by a toss from the back of a bronc.

The notion was crazy, he told himself. Even more crazy than Virginia's idea of a time warp. Why, he reasoned, would the Almighty fling him over a hundred years into the future? Then again, what was time to God?

In much the same manner as had happened that night, old, forgotten words whispered through his mind. He didn't know if the words were complete or in their proper order, but they settled the issue for him, just the same.

The Lord works in strange and mysterious ways.

Matt was still sitting on the bed, pondering strange and mysterious ways, when his introspection was interrupted by a light rap against the door, followed by the soft, beguiling sound of Virginia's voice.

"Matt, may I come in?"

"Sure," he replied, in a laconic tone that belied the excitement shimmering inside him. He was standing beside the bed when she entered, an inquisitive expression on his face and a feeling of possessiveness in his soul.

"Settled in?" Her smile tore a chunk out of his heart.

"Who's Richard?" Matt asked the question that had been simmering beneath his surface thoughts.

Virginia's smile dimmed, just a mite. "A friend."

Matt raised his brows. "A special friend?" His tone deliberately suggested intimacy.

"I beg your pardon?" Her smile vanished.

"You know what I mean," Matt chided softly.

The warmth drained from her beautiful eyes. "No," Virginia said in a cool, distant tone. "I'm afraid you'll have to spell it out for me."

Matt was suddenly positive his suspicions were correct, but he wasn't at all sure he wanted to hear them confirmed. Still, some inner, green-eyed demon had to know. "I mean," he said with soft emphasis, "have you been together?"

"In the biblical sense?" she asked in frigid tones.

Matt exploded. "Yes, dammit!"

Virginia raised her chin and looked him squarely in the eyes. "That, Mr. Hawk, is none of your damn business."

His steps slow, Matt advanced on her. "I'm making it my business." As he moved forward, she retreated, until her back made contact with the door. He caged her there by planting his hands against the panel on either side. "Now," he murmured when she was trapped, "have you been with him?"

Helpless but clearly undaunted, Virginia continued to hold his gaze and glared at him in apparent fearlessness. He'd respected her before and now the sense deepened. "You are a guest in my home," she said bitingly. "You have no right whatever to question me about my love life or anything else."

"Oh, but I do have that right, Virginia," Matt corrected her, lowering his head to brush his mouth over hers. The fact that her response was evidently against her will sent shards of candescent pleasure to every inch of his body, a pleasure deepened by the breathless quality of her voice.

"By what right?" she demanded.

"Oh, didn't you know?" Matt lifted his head to smile at her. "You are God's answer to my Christmas prayer."

Seven

"What did you say?" Virginia asked, positive she hadn't heard what she thought she'd heard.

"I said I have the right, because you are God's answer to my Christmas prayer," Matt repeated.

"That's what I thought you said," she muttered, thinking that perhaps she should have consulted the psychiatrist, after all. "But you don't really believe that," she went on hopefully. "Do you?"

"Sure," Matt drawled. "It's the only explanation that makes any sense."

"Well, it doesn't make sense to me!" she cried. "Why would you believe that?"

"You remember I told you I was on my way to church when I was shot?" He raised his head a few inches to look into her wary eyes.

"Yes, I remember, but—"

"But wait," Matt cut in. "I didn't tell you all of it."
He paused, his eyes cloudy with recollection. "I
thought I was a goner for sure.... No, I knew I was
dying." He shook his head. "And I knew I wasn't
going to get another chance, a chance for a decent life,
a place of my own, a woman of my own." His eyes
cleared, glittering with inner conviction. "Right before I passed out, I called out to God, telling him I
couldn't die." He stared into her widened eyes with a
drilling intensity. "When I came to, you were the first
thing I saw." He smiled. "At first I thought you were
an angel. Now I believe that you were God's answer to
my dying prayer."

A spasm of unease flickered in Virginia's stomach
as the precariousness of her position hit her. She was
trapped in a bedroom with a man who believed she
had been given to him in answer to his prayers. The
added realization that the merest brush of his mouth
over her own sent desire racing through her certainly
didn't improve her lot. What if he decided to claim
her—here and now?

The thought had an unnerving effect on Virginia.
The uneasy feeling in her stomach flared into a blaze
of excited anticipation. Her senses went wild, demanding...all kinds of tempting but forbidden plea-
sures. The very intensity of her involuntary response
alerted her more rational, controlling common sense.

Pull it together, Doctor, Virginia advised herself,
infusing strength into her weakened spine. Retain
professional distance. You cannot afford to become
emotionally involved in a situation that's already too
bizarre to be believed. He's lost. Don't get lost with

him. And the first order of business is to get yourself out of the bedroom!

Acting on her own excellent advice, she assumed her best bedside manner. "What makes you so certain that I'm the answer to your prayer?"

"I told you," he said. "It's the only thing that makes any sense."

Virginia bit back an impatient retort in favor of a more reasonable reply. "But you see, it doesn't make sense to me. I don't understand. I want you to explain it to me."

"I want to kiss you."

"I don't think that would be wise," she said, talking to herself as well as to him. She was the only one listening; he was staring intently at her mouth.

"Ginnie, I need to kiss you." His breath whispered over her lips as he brought his mouth closer.

Virginia's blood raced in time with her heartbeat. Her pulse leaped and her throat went dry. Pressing the back of her head against the door, she shook it slowly, denying him, denying herself. "Matt, listen to me." Her voice was reedy, almost nonexistent. "I think we must talk about—"

"I think you talk too much," he murmured, silencing her with his mouth.

Virginia resisted the temptation of his hungry kiss for all of three seconds. Then her inner resources dissolved. Giving in to her own need, she surrendered to the irresistible allure of the hard mouth and body pressing against her. Raising her arms, she curled them around his waist. Trembling from the riot of sensations that were racing through her, she clung to him, absorbing his heat and hard strength, drowning in his taste.

His broad hands clasped her hips, aligning them to his own. Virginia gasped when he arched his body, making her aware of the need and passion she had aroused in him. She moaned low in her throat, when he thrust his tongue into her mouth, simulating a more complete possession.

She was on fire, and so was he. Virginia could feel his heated skin through the soft material of his shirt. She couldn't breathe, she couldn't think...and she didn't care. She didn't want to think, didn't even want to breathe; she wanted his kiss to go on for ever. He began to move; she moved with him. It was then that Virginia realized that he was trembling, too. She blinked and murmured a soft protest when he broke the kiss.

"Ginnie, come to bed with me." Matt's voice was raspy and his forehead was beaded with moisture. But it was the pallor beneath his sun-weathered skin that brought Virginia to her senses.

"Matt, are you in pain?" Snapping back into her role of physician, Virginia raised her palm to his face.

"I'm all right," he said, pulling away from her hand. "Or at least I will be, if you come to bed with me."

Even with only that brief touch, she had felt the fever in him sear her palm. "No, Matt. You're going to bed, but you're going alone," Virginia said decisively. "You've been under great strain, and your wound is not completely hea—" she broke off in alarm when he winced. "What is it? Are you in—?

Matt!'' she exclaimed as his arms suddenly dropped to his sides.

He tried to smile, but it came off as a grimace. ''Shoulder hurts like hell.'' He took several quick, deep breaths. ''I don't know,'' he said, shaking his head. ''I feel kinda funny.''

Slipping one arm around his waist, Virginia guided him to the side of the bed. ''There's nothing funny about it,'' she said, yanking back the spread and covers with her free hand. ''I think you'd better lie down before you fall down.''

Running true to character, Matt resisted her efforts to help him onto the bed. ''I'll be all right in a minute. I just need to catch my breath.''

The emotional upheaval he had put her through, immediately followed by anxiety, took their toll on Virginia's nerves and patience. ''Dammit, Matt, get into that bed!'' she ordered, giving him a gentle shove.

Matt rocked on his feet but remained standing. ''I will, if you'll lay down with me.'' He clenched his teeth and set his jaw at a determined angle.

Virginia's already frayed nerves were beginning to unravel. Silently railing against his obstinancy, yet reluctantly admiring his strength of purpose, she glared at him in mounting frustration. ''Matt, listen to me,'' she said with soft entreaty. ''You need to rest.''

''I need you with me, beside me.''

She could have withstood defiance or even belligerence, but against the forlorn note woven through his low voice she was defenseless. Virginia surrendered with a sigh. ''All right, but it's time for your medication,'' she said, referring to the antibiotic she had prescribed to ward off infection. "You get undressed and get into bed, while I get it for you."

Matt caught her hand as she turned away. "You promise you'll come back?" His palm was hot and dry.

"Yes, of course I'll be back." She tugged against his hold, discovering how weak he really was when her fingers slipped free of his limp hand. "Do you need help undressing?"

He shook his head. "No, I need you," he muttered.

"I'll hurry," she promised, concern charging her with energy. Striding from the room, she went in search of her handbag, in which she had stashed his medication before they'd left the hospital. She found it exactly where she had set it down, on the kitchen table.

Moments later, carrying a glass of water, the antibiotic and two aspirin to combat his fever, Virginia reentered the room. She found Matt, clad now in cotton undershirt and shorts, seated on the side of the bed, his face strained from the effort of removing his boots. Crossing to him, she thrust the water glass in front of him with one hand and pushed him upright with the other.

"Here, you take these," she instructed, opening her hand to show him the capsule and aspirin. "I'll take care of those." She inclined her head to indicate the boots.

Virginia found the chore easier said than done...for more reasons than the simple fact that his boots resisted the tug of her hands. There was an element of distraction, and that element made her feel as fever-ish as he was.

Matt's jeans were bunched around the tops of his boots. His long legs were bare. His briefs were... brief... and molded to his manhood. While yanking ineffectually on his boots, Virginia trailed a glance up the length of his pale-skinned, dark-haired legs. She noted the tremors of fatigue rippling the long, solid muscles of his thighs, then stared in arrested fascina-tion at the narrow scrap of navy blue cotton swathing his hips. She had no idea how long she had been star-ing, or how much longer she would have continued to do so, when her trancelike state was broken by the movement of his arm as he raised the glass to his lips to swallow the pills. Heat rushing to her head, Vir-ginia pulled her gaze back to his boots.

What in heaven's name was wrong with her? she chastised herself scathingly, yanking at the footgear with renewed force. She had seen all manner of men stark naked, young, old, stout, slender, without bat-ting an eyelash. She was a physician, a professional, and the last time she had flushed or felt uncomfort-able about viewing the unadorned human form was in her second year of medical school. Yet now, with this one man, this obstreperous, demanding man, she fell apart, becoming all hot and squishy inside.

Ridiculous! An angry yank and the first boot pulled free.

Ludicrous! Another yank and the second boot joined its partner on the floor.

But true. Exhausted, Virginia flopped back onto the floor next to the boots.

"Thanks." Matt heaved a tired sigh and offered her a weak smile. "I was beginning to think I'd have to sleep with the damn things on."

"It plays hell with the sheets," Virginia retorted, smiling back at him.

"You're picking up my bad habit, Doc," he chided her, slowly raising a hand to rake his fingers through his long, shaggy hair. "But that's okay, I still like you." His eyelids drooping, he fell back and stretched his length on the bed. A blissful-sounding sigh escaped his slightly parted lips. "Get out of your clothes and come to bed, Ginnie. I need you beside me." Still suffering embarrassment over her unaccustomed reaction to his nearly nude body, she was on the point of refusing, when he demolished her will by appealing to her sympathy. "I'm cold and lonely."

Virginia was a qualified diagnostician. Judging by his symptoms, she was fairly certain that Matt would be physically unable to present a problem to her if she crawled into bed with him. But Virginia was wary, as well, and there was no way she was about to undress before getting into bed beside him—whether or not he was weak and running a fever.

She hesitated for a moment, then cast a rueful glance at her skirt and crisp, shirt-style blouse. Without a doubt the material would be crushed. Lifting her shoulders in a tired shrug, she scrambled up off the floor and onto the bed. Rather the skirt and blouse than herself.

Matt slung his good arm around her an instant after she slid onto the mattress next to him. Virginia went as stiff as a board. Mumbling her name, he drew her close, and tightening his hold, anchored her there.

His body radiated a dry, burning heat. Compassion and another, more intimidating, emotion drained the resistance from her.

"Go to sleep, Matthew Hawk, United States marshal from the nineteenth century," she murmured, brushing the tousled curls from his face with a gentle touch. "Virginia Greyson, liberated woman physician of the twentieth century will watch over you."

Smiling at her unusual whimsy, Virginia cradled Matt's shivering body in her arms and pressed her soft lips to his moist brow. Within minutes, their bodies entwined, both Matt and Virginia were sound asleep.

It was late afternoon when the screech of tires on the parking lot beneath the bedroom window woke Virginia. Darkness had already settled in. For a moment, disoriented and feeling somewhat smothered, she didn't know where she was. A gentle snore near the top of her head brought memory rushing back.

Her first thought was for Matt. He appeared to be in a deep, restful sleep. The heat of high fever no longer radiated from his relaxed body. Virginia felt the skin on his face and neck with a feather-light touch of her hand. It was cool. Holding her breath, she slipped free of the lax, heavy weight of the arm he had draped around her waist and the leg he had flung across her thigh. Matt grunted, but slept on. Sighing with relief, she tiptoed from the room.

Though her skirt and blouse indeed looked dead, a shower brought Virginia's mind and body back to life. Revived, she pulled on a cherry-red cotton knit sweater and black straight-legged jeans, then stepped into fur-lined house moccasins. Leaving her skin to breathe without makeup, she gave her hair a vigorous brushing, tossed the crackling mane off her shoulders, and left her bedroom in search of something to appease her complaining stomach.

Canned soup was heating on the stove, and Virginia was slicing cold chicken for sandwiches, when the unexpected sound of Matt's voice jolted her. She gasped and jumped. The sharp knife missed her finger by a hair.

"You're wearing men's pants!" he exclaimed in a sleepy voice.

Dropping the knife to the countertop, Virginia whirled to confront him. "For heaven's sake, Matt, you startled me so badly, I nearly amputated my finger!"

"Dammit, Ginnie, you're wearing men's pants," he repeated, as if her attire held priority over her person.

Virginia rolled her eyes, then swept her gaze down the front of her body. "Well, darned if I'm not," she muttered in exaggerated astonishment. She raised her eyes to give him a wry look, and felt her senses swim from the impact of the way *he* looked. He was fresh from the shower, his hair still wet, long strands curling down the back of his neck and over the collar of his shirt. The taut skin of his face wore the sheen of health and a smooth shave. Coincidentally, he too was wearing black jeans but with a red and black plaid shirt. The overall effect his appearance had on her equilibrium didn't bear thinking about—so she dragged her thoughts back to the conversation.

"This is the twentieth century, Matt. Women wear pants all the time." Virginia's throat went dry, and her voice grew uneven before she'd finished speaking. For while she was studying him, he had obviously been inspecting her, and his hooded eyes were plainly measuring the circumference of her breasts.

"You look good in red." His voice was low, sexy, suggesting the thoughts multiplying in his mind. His long fingers flexed, as if in readiness to confirm his mental calculations.

Virginia's legs trembled and seemed on the point of quitting their job of supporting her body. Her breathing appeared ready to go on strike. "Ah...thank you." She drew a quick breath and uttered a silent moan at the revealing huskiness of her voice.

"Ginnie." Murmuring her name, Matt took a step toward her, then stopped dead, his head snapping up alertly when the phone rang. He stood watching her as she walked to the instrument, mounted on the opposite wall. "More than likely that Richard person again," he muttered.

Virginia hoped he was wrong. She didn't want to speak to Richard, not after the argument he had initiated with her during his earlier call. He had insisted on stopping by to talk to her, and she had had a hard time convincing him that she was too busy to see him. There was a confrontation brewing, and Virginia knew it. She also knew she wasn't up to it at the moment.

Fortunately it wasn't Richard. When she lifted the receiver, Jeff Klein responded to her cautious greeting.

"Oh, hello, Jeff," she said on a sigh of relief. Matt scowled. She ignored him. "Have you learned anything?"

"Not much," Jeff replied. "He's not wanted any-where. In fact, the only information either Washing-ton or Fort Worth could come up with on a Matthew Hawk was an old record on a U.S. marshal by that name. But that record dates back to 1889, the year the marshal disappeared, presumed murdered in Mon-tana by the outlaw he was after." Jeff sounded baf-fled. "As for this Matthew Hawk, who may or may not be a descendant of the marshal, they can't come up with a thing, no social security number, no service record, nothing, zilch. As far as the authorities are concerned, he doesn't even exist."

It was true! Virginia thought. Every word Matt had said about himself was true. Shaken by the realiza-tion, she had to exert every ounce of willpower she possessed to maintain her composure long enough to ask one final question.

"And as far as you're concerned?"

"He doesn't exist."

Virginia held herself together until she had thanked Jeff and hung up the receiver. Then, trembling with reaction, she closed her eyes. She didn't hear Matt move on his stockinged feet, but an instant later felt the support of the arm he slid around her waist.

"Ginnie, what's wrong?" he demanded in a tone laced with anger and concern. "What did that man say to you?"

She drew in a deep breath to restore her sense of balance, and immediately wished she hadn't. The clean male scent of him went straight to her head. Needing distance from him, room to breathe, Vir-ginia stepped away from his protective hold and walked to the stove.

"That man was Jeff Klein, one of the patrolmen at the scene the night you were . . . found," she told him. "He called to tell me the results of the record check he requested on you from Washington and Fort Worth."

"And?" Matt's very stillness betrayed his sudden tension.

Virginia relayed the information Jeff had given to her. When she finished, she stared at him as if he were a ghost. "It's true, Matt. You were shot in Montana in 1889, and somehow wound up here, in Pennsylvania, in the twentieth century."

Matt was silent for a moment, then he started moving toward her, a slow, satisfied smile curving his lips. "I told you that you were God's answer to my prayer—didn't I?" He arched his brows over eyes gleaming with purpose.

His remark reverberating in her mind, she watched him closing the space between them. The full meaning of his words registered as he drew within reaching distance. Matt actually believed she was his by divine decree!

"Ah . . . supper!" Coming to her senses, she spun around, grabbed a spoon and gave the bubbling soup a frantic stir. "I don't know about you, but I'm starving."

"Yes, I'm hungry."

Something, some sly, sensuous something about his low tone drew her around to face him again. Passion glittered in his eyes. A faint but blatantly wicked smiled teased the corners of his mouth. Virginia didn't need to have his meaning explained—he took care of that.

"I could eat something, too."

The man was impossible! Virginia thought wildly. And she was a wreck. When did she lose control of this situation? she asked herself, stirring the soup for all it was worth. When did you ever have control of the situation? her inner self responded—and why are you beating the innocent soup?

Shaking away the thoughts, she glanced down just in time to see the hot liquid slosh over the rim of the saucepan. As she listened to the broth sizzle on the electric coil, her lips set into a straight line. She switched off the burner, and determination rang in her voice when she turned to confront her tormentor.

"I can offer you canned soup and cold chicken sandwiches," she said firmly.

Matt wasn't slow on the uptake. His expression revealed perfect understanding. Still, he gave it another shot. "No dessert?"

Virginia expelled a harsh, impatient sigh. "Butter pound cake."

"That's it?"

"That's it," she repeated with a note of finality. "Take it or leave it."

Matt shrugged. "I'll take it." Then he grinned. "There's always tomorrow."

"Not if you want a roof over your head," Virginia said through gritted teeth.

His eyebrows shot up. "What do you mean?"

"I'll give you the house rules over supper."

While she sipped her soup and toyed with a sandwich, Virginia enumerated the rules. Making them up as she went along, she instructed him in the proper behavior of a guest—at least a guest in *her* home. Of course, since she was beginning to fear that she couldn't trust herself, she dumped the responsibility onto his shoulders. The bottom line was, naturally, that Matt was to make no further suggestive remarks or overt moves directed at her person.

"In other words, keep your hands to yourself," she concluded. "Or you will find yourself out on the street, on your own in a world, I might remind you, that you know nothing about." Finished, she met his disconcerted stare. "Agreed?"

"Why, Ginnie?" Matt frowned in confusion. "You couldn't get enough of me, my mouth, before. If I hadn't had that weak spell we'd have been all over each other in that bed, and you know it. What's changed since then?"

Being reminded of her eager responses to his kiss brought a flush of heat to her face, but Virginia managed to keep her tone detached and cool. "My professional opinion is that my response to you earlier was simply a reaction to the stress incurred by the unusual circumstances surrounding your sudden appearance in my life." Even to herself, the explanation sounded like a load of intellectual gibberish. Nevertheless, she babbled on. "And now that the stress valve has been released, the buildup of excess emotions has dissipated."

"Which means exactly what?" he asked tersely.

"I lost my head for a moment," she admitted.

Matt looked confounded. "But you enjoyed it every bit as much as I did. Why not—?"

She didn't let him finish. "I don't have time in my life for emotional involvement, Matt." Before he had a chance to question her, she rushed into an explanation. "Ever since I can remember, all I wanted was to be a doctor, a surgeon, to help people, hopefully to cure them. My schedule is tight. My life is full and satisfying. I neither need nor want a man cluttering up my life and messing with my concentration."

"What about that man you were talking to before?" he retorted. "That Richard somebody?"

"Richard is a friend, nothing more." The thought flashed into her head that she needed to make that clear to Richard, also. "And his last name is Quinter."

"Can't I be your friend, too?"

Matt's wistfully muttered request not only surprised Virginia, it almost undermined her resolve. Matt was so utterly alone. She fully understood his desire to attach himself to someone. But she couldn't be that someone; she couldn't afford to allow herself to become involved with him. Her reaction to him was too strong, too intense. She had to keep her distance, keep him at arm's length. Her independence depended on it.

Denying an urge to reach across the table and grasp his hand, she offered him a smile instead. "Of course we can be friends," she said, but added quickly, "as long as you remember that friends don't pressure one another."

Matt obviously wasn't satisfied with her reply, but he nodded his agreement. "I don't have much choice, do I?"

"No, you don't."

Though he had agreed to play by her rules, his eyes had a cloudy, stormy look. He finished eating his meal, and then the storm broke. Exhaling harshly, he exclaimed, "Dammit, Ginnie, what am I going to do all day while you're away from the place, keeping your tight schedule?''

"Do you read?''

"I'm not uneducated! I went to school!'' Matt exploded. "Of course I can read.''

Virginia sighed. "I didn't ask you if you *can* read, Matt,'' she said. "I asked you if you *do* read.'' She gave him a tolerant smile. "There's a difference, you know.''

Matt had the grace to at least appear chastised. "Oh, yeah,'' he muttered. "I do like to read, although I never had the time or the books to do much of it. Why?''

"Why?'' Virginia repeated. "Why, because, in case you hadn't noticed, there are all kinds of books in my den,'' she pointed out in a dry tone. "And since you have over a hundred years of history to catch up on, I'd say you have plenty to do while I'm working.''

His latest ploy thwarted, Matt slumped against the back of his chair. "Well, from where I'm sitting,'' he grumbled, "I'd say it looks like it's going to be a long, cold winter.''

Eight

——

Though the snowfall from a late-winter storm the week before still covered the ground, the scent and feel of spring was in the air. The sunshine was warm, the breeze balmy, lifting the spirits of the winter-weary residents.

His shoulder completely healed, Matt loped along the sidewalk, his step light in his latest acquisition. Virginia called them jogging shoes. He called them comfortable...and expensive. He had become aware of current prices the first time he had gone shopping with Virginia. Fortunately, due to the mind-boggling amount of cash Virginia had received from a collector for his gold coins, Matt could now pay for his own purchases. The cost of jogging shoes had come as a shock to him; the shock had still not completely worn off, but he did enjoy walking in the comfortable footgear.

The low-cut shoes, so different from the heeled boots that made extended walking difficult, were a minor revelation in comparison to the startling information he had absorbed over the past three months.

Early in the New Year Matt had begun walking, exploring the town of Conifer and its environs, after Virginia had returned to work when her ten-day holiday was over. He had learned a lot during the intervening weeks, about life and history as well as about the small town in the mountains of Pennsylvania.

"Afternoon, ma'am." Matt smiled, raised his hand to give a respectful tug to the wide brim of his hat, and stepped aside, close to the snow banked at the curb. The middle-aged woman who was passing him looked startled for an instant, then tentatively returned both smile and greeting.

His smile turned wry as he continued on his way. He had grown accustomed to the initial hesitation of most folks to respond to a stranger. And, though Christmas was long past, Matt was still a stranger, not only to the town and its residents, but to the twentieth century.

But he was making definite progress. He no longer stiffened at the sudden, shrill ring of the telephone or the unexpected blare of a car horn. He didn't duck reflexively at the sound of a plane overhead. On the contrary, he now spoke on the phone with Virginia as though he'd been doing so all his life, and was eagerly looking forward to getting behind the wheel of a car and to his first flight in a plane...preferably in one of the big jets he had read about.

He had solved the intriguing mysteries of working the automatic washer and dryer, the dishwasher, the microwave and the VCR, and was learning the intricacies of the personal computer. Most days when he walked, it was with the earphones to Virginia's tiny cassette player clamped to his head—beneath the restored Stetson that Virginia had had cleaned and blocked, when he'd refused even to consider wearing any other hat. And he had had his long shaggy hair trimmed—not lopped off, he wouldn't even consider anything above the ears—by a stylist, no less. In addition to all the other radical changes in his life, he had quit smoking, thanks in part to Virginia's opinion on the habit, but due mostly to his dissatisfaction with both premade cigarettes and the tasteless version of the modern makin's.

To Virginia's surprise, Matt favored rock music over country and western—even though he liked C and W. But his real favorites were her tapes of classical music, and he was hooked on TV and history books, both factual and fictional.

The events that had occurred since 1889 astounded Matt, most particularly the happenings and inventions of the latter half of the twentieth century. He found it incredible that from the beginning of recorded history, including his own time, most men had never set foot in an automobile, and yet within the short span of less than a hundred years, man had gone soaring through space to set foot upon the moon.

In Matt's opinion, people, by and large, had not changed all that much. He believed as he had before that the majority of people were basically decent. But, as before, there were the aberrants, those who chose for whatever reason to walk on the wild side, living outside the accepted boundaries of the law. His greatest disappointment was in the discovery that, to all intents and purposes, law enforcement had not changed very much.... It was still the good guys against the bad, the shoot-out at the OK corral, except that the weapons were far more sophisticated.

To Matt it was all rather overwhelming and confusing, while at the same time exciting and stimulating. There was also one other great disappointment. He and Virginia had read everything on the theory of time travel that she had been able to unearth at the lending library and in bookstores. There had been relatively little concrete information to garner, for the books available on the subject were primarily from the romance genre, interesting and imaginative, but hardly scientific in approach. So, although Virginia continued to search for other material on the subject, they had both resigned themselves to the prospect of never finding anything really enlightening.

To a certain extent, the days never seemed quite long enough, packed full as they were with new things to do and learn about. In addition to his pursuit of knowledge, he had acquired skills in activities he had never before dreamed of attempting.

Determined to "earn his keep," as he termed it to Virginia, Matt had taken over the housework. He had become proficient at doing the laundry and keeping the place tidy, and was even a fair-to-middlin' cook. He did not feel in the least demeaned by performing the chores—possibly because no one had told him the work was beneath him. Virginia was pleased with the arrangement, and that in itself was incentive enough for Matt.

But, as he had predicted the day Virginia brought him from the hospital to her apartment, it had still been a long, cold winter.

Matt was oblivious to the display of pastel-hued spring merchandise in shop windows as he strode along the town's main street. Inside his mind visions rose, replaying fragments of incidents that had occurred during the previous weeks.

"Now watch carefully," Virginia had instructed him. "When the apple gets to the base of the pole, the crowd will go a little crazy."

They were seated side by side on the sofa, watching a TV special event. Virginia had purchased a bottle of champagne for the occasion. Sipping the wine—a new and delicious experience for him—Matt kept his gaze trained on the screen. When the apple reached the base of the pole and a sign reading Happy New Year flashed on, his interest sharpened. It wasn't the noise and revelry that riveted his attention as much as the fact that everybody was kissing everybody else.

"Why are they doing that?" he'd asked, switching his gaze from the TV to the woman beside him.

Virginia had looked a trifle flustered, but had replied, "Kissing has become the traditional way of welcoming in the New Year."

"I think I like it." Smiling, he had set his glass aside and reached for her.

"Matt, remember what I said about keeping your hands to yourself." Frowning, she had shaken her head and tried to avoid his arms.

He was faster than she. He caught her by the shoulders as she started to bolt from the sofa. "Can't afford to break with tradition," he'd murmured, ignoring the twinge of pain in his shoulder as he drew her into his arms. "Might bring a whole year of bad luck."

After her initial resistance, the kiss they shared had been long, deep and hot to the point of sizzling. Aching for her with every cell in his being, he had glided one hand around her midriff and up to the enticing fullness of one breast. The feel of her warmed his palm and set his body on fire. Needing, wanting, he'd deepened the kiss by thrusting his tongue into the honeyed depths of her mouth. Aroused and bemused by the sweet wonders of her mouth and body, Matt had dropped his guard—and Virginia had seized the moment to make good her escape.

The memory of that searing, blatantly sensuous kiss, more intoxicating than the wine, had tormented Matt throughout every cold, empty night since then. There had been no repeat performance. While his body burned with desire to be a part of her, Virginia had kept her distance.

Matt's lips tightened as another vision sprang into his mind, a memory of the unpleasant scene that had taken place the evening Richard Quinter had appeared, uninvited and unexpected, at her door.

"Why, Richard! What are you doing here?"

Matt had heard Virginia's surprised response to the visitor from the den, where he was puzzling over a computer program instruction book, which was written in the foreign language she called "computerese."

At the sound of the visitor's name, he'd set the book aside.

"I should think the answer would be obvious," Richard had replied in a superior tone of voice that Matt immediately took exception to. His eyes narrowed as the man continued. "I came to see you, of course. And to find out why you've been avoiding me for over a month."

"Richard, please, I don't want to discuss this now. I'm—" That was as far as he'd allowed her to go.

"I thought we had an understanding," Richard said, cutting her off in an overbearing way.

"Richard, I never—" Virginia had begun again, only to be rudely interrupted once more.

"You never dated any other man. I, my parents, all our friends considered us a couple." His voice had taken on a definite note of ownership—and Matt had felt his anger begin to rise.

"We were never a couple," Virginia had corrected the unexpected visitor, sighing in exasperation. "I tried to explain this to you when we spoke on the phone at Christmas."

"You said your patient came first," Richard had retorted. "I assumed your patient was either cured or dead by now," he'd added nastily.

Matt had heard enough. His movements noiseless, he ambled out of the den and into the living room. "Trouble, honey?" he'd drawled. While Richard stared at him in astonished disbelief, Matt strolled to Virginia and slipped an arm around her waist in a manner both familiar and possessive.

Taking her cue like a trained actress, Virginia had smiled, moved closer to him and murmured, "Not at all, darling. Richard just stopped by to say hello."

"Then I suggest he say goodbye," Matt had replied, treating the other man to a cold smile and an even colder, lethal stare. "It's time for bed."

Richard had fallen for the performance. Looking insulted and offended, he'd swept a look of disgust over Virginia, then turned and stormed away.

Virginia had slipped out of Matt's encircling arm the minute the door closed behind the other man. Her color high, her voice dangerously low, she had then proceeded to give Matt royal hell for his interference. He had listened for a moment, then interrupted her.

"He's a shadow rider."

Angrier than he had ever seen her, Virginia had glared at him and demanded, "What in hell is a shadow rider?"

Amused by her growing tendency to swear when she was riled, Matt had hidden his smile and explained. "A shadow rider is the term used to describe a vain cowboy, a man so impressed with himself, he might find his own shadow attractive." He'd arched his brows. "The term fits Richard like his expensive suit...doesn't it?"

Virginia had held her stern expression for several seconds, then burst out laughing. "Yes," she'd admitted. "The term fits him to perfection."

The memory brought a smile to Matt's lips and lightened his loping stride. There were moments when he missed the creak of saddle leather and the feel of a horse beneath him, but those moments were growing fewer and farther between. All things considered, he knew he was adjusting well to the shock of finding himself in this sometimes incomprehensible, yet exciting new environment.

Given the choice between returning to his own time or remaining in the twentieth century, Matt knew without doubt that he'd choose to stay where he was. Even with pollution, the fear of the greenhouse effect, international tensions and the specter of nuclear devastation, he much preferred the convenience and comfort of the present. Because, most important of all his considerations, Virginia resided in the present.

Virginia.

Matt was suffused with a warmth unrelated to the bright sunshine. Thinking about her never failed to warm him. Being around her never failed to set his mind and body on fire. He was in love with her. Matt accepted his love for Virginia without question or doubt.

By the grace of God or not, Matt now knew, intellectually and emotionally, that Virginia belonged to him. He knew as well that he belonged to her. To his way of thinking, his mystical slip through time had had to happen, for they were surely destined to be together.

The long winter of confinement within her apartment had proven their compatibility to him. They were both strong, determined, and basically loners, and yet they had coped, not only well but smoothly with the necessity of sharing their space. At times they had clashed, as would be expected of two strong-willed individuals, but those incidents were few in number compared to the times they had laughed together, as they had on the night Richard had stormed off in a huff.

Turning a corner at an intersection, Matt quickened his pace. After three months, he now knew the route by heart. He was headed home. And to Matt, home meant Virginia . . . in any century.

Letting himself into the apartment with the key she'd had made for him, Matt shrugged out of the parka, then went directly to the kitchen. Even though Virginia spent little time in it, the place always felt empty when she wasn't there. After switching on the radio to dispel the silence, he began gathering the ingredients needed for a casserole for dinner. With his thoughts his only company, he prepared the dish, slid it into the oven, then glanced around, looking for something else to do to occupy his time. There was nothing; everything was neat and orderly. He looked at the clock and sighed. Virginia wouldn't be home for at least another hour.

Restless, he ambled into the living room and to the wide window overlooking the foothills at the rear of the apartment complex. In his opinion, Virginia worked too hard and relaxed too seldom. Scanning the snow-covered scene beyond the window, Matt's gaze came to rest on the clearing in a stand of pines. A smile relieved the tightness of his lips as he studied the results of one of her too few periods of relaxation.

The snowman certainly wasn't a work of art, but he and Virginia had laughed a lot together while building it after the storm earlier that week.

Together. The word revolving in his mind, Matt pulled on his jacket and left the apartment. Moments later he was in the clearing, scooping up snow to shore up the drooping snowman . . . Virginia's snowman.

Virginia and he belonged together, were fated to be together. He knew it. His problem was in convincing her of it. Matt worked on the problem while he worked on the snowman.

Virginia parked her car in her designated slot in the parking lot at the apartment complex. It was still light! The realization struck her as she walked toward the entrance of her building. Spring had arrived, the daylight hours were growing longer, and she hadn't noticed until that minute. Of course, she was earlier than usual. By some stroke of luck, her last two scheduled patients had both called to cancel their appointments.

Closing her eyes, Virginia inhaled deeply. Yes, the unmistakable scent of spring was in the cooling afternoon air. The scent permeated her being, inducing a heady feeling. The scent? she chided herself. Or the man waiting for her inside the building?

Matt. His name teased her senses, causing a much more potent headiness than any scent of spring. Matt was waiting for her. Anticipation shimmering through her, she entered the building and hurried to the elevator. After a scant three months of having him at the apartment, Virginia couldn't imagine him not being there, waiting for her.

She was in love with him, of course. After a fierce inner battle, Virginia had finally admitted to herself the reality of the love she felt for him. It scared her witless. Falling in love wasn't in her life plan. She loved her work, her independence, her freedom. She didn't want to be in love with any man, most especially not with a man from another, earlier century.

And Matt had proved himself a man of his time. He was tough, rugged, and not above turning a situation to his own advantage, as he had on New Year's Eve and again on the night Richard had suddenly appeared at her door.

The thought of the latter incident brought a smile to Virginia's lips. The memory of the former occasion sent a shiver skipping down her spine. Nearly three months had passed, during which she had carefully avoided any form of physical contact with him, yet she could still taste him, still feel the heat and urgency of his mouth and hands.

It was enough to make a strong-minded woman weep. She didn't want to be in love with Matthew Hawk. She didn't want to feel the quickening of her pulse whenever she thought about him or he drew within scenting distance of her. Still, while Virginia's mind resisted, her emotions sent her rushing from the elevator and into the apartment.

The tantalizing aroma of simmering food enveloped Virginia the moment she stepped over the threshold. Smiling in appreciation of Matt's growing culinary skill, she followed the scent to its source in the kitchen. Expecting to find the creator of the meal, she frowned when all she found was an empty room. In fact, the entire apartment was empty. Matt wasn't there.

Wondering where he could have gone, Virginia went to her bedroom to change out of her attractive but subdued suit and into her more comfortable jeans and pullover sweater. There was still no sign of him when she left her room fifteen minutes later.

Thinking that perhaps he had decided to take a short nap, she went to his room. The door was open. His room was as empty as all the others. Strangely uneasy, Virginia drifted aimlessly from one room to another. Where was he? she asked herself, becoming anxious. He was always there when she got home. It wasn't like Matt to disappear this late in the afternoon, not even to run out to the sto—

Virginia's thoughts shattered. *Disappear.* The word echoed in her mind. A flashing memory left her feeling as cold and empty as her apartment. The memory was of one of the time travel novels she and Matt had read. In the story, the heroine, from another time period, had in the end, without warning, suddenly disappeared.

It was fiction, Virginia reminded herself, clasping her arms around her trembling body. But what if? . . . *Stop this at once,* she ordered herself. Attempting to escape her own churning thoughts, she retraced her steps, pacing from room to room. At the open doorway to Matt's bedroom she came to a halt. A wrenching pain of loss tore a cry from her throat. She loved him, and if he was gone, lost to her, he would never know.

"Matt." Virginia was unaware of calling his name aloud. Frantic, frightened, she turned away. What would she do if he had just disappeared, like a puff of smoke in a stiff breeze? she asked herself. How could she bear the emptiness of whatever remained of her life?

At that moment, Virginia would have given everything she valued—her work, her independence, her freedom—for the sound of his voice, his laughter.

Feeling lost, bereft, she wandered into the living room. The delicious aroma of the meal he had prepared wafted to her once more from the kitchen. Tears filled her eyes, blurring her vision. Chafing her shivering arms, she walked to the window. The day was losing the light. It would soon be as dark outside as she felt inside. Remembering their snowman, she wiped the tears from her eyes and raised her head to look at the clearing.

"Matt!" This time his name exploded from her throat. As real as life and twice as beautiful, Matt was in the clearing, shoring up their melting snowman.

Virginia was absolutely still for an instant, devouring the sight of him. Relief and sheer joy washed over her, bringing a smile to her lips and wings to her feet. Spinning around, she ran to the closet. Grabbing her ski parka, she pulled it on as she dashed from the apartment.

"Matt," Virginia called to him as she raced from the complex to the clearing. He turned and waved.

"Hi," he responded, smiling with evident pleasure. "You're early, aren't you?"

"Yes," she replied, coming to a halt in front of him. "Two appointments canceled." Flushed and breathless, she gazed into his eyes and blurted out her fears. "I couldn't find you. I was worried."

The crease lines at the corners of his eyes crinkled when he laughed. "Afraid I'd skipped with the silver?"

"No." Virginia was powerless against the emotions roiling inside her and the tears that rushed to her eyes. "I was afraid you were...gone," she whispered.

Matt frowned. His brilliant eyes searched her face. "Gone? Gone where?"

"Back." Virginia sniffed, and didn't even care. Matt obviously did care.

"Ginnie, you're crying!" he exclaimed, pulling her into his arms. "What is it? What's wrong?" he demanded. "And what do you mean by 'back'?"

Sobbing, she flung her arms around his neck and held him fast. She didn't care that they were in view of the other residents of the complex. She didn't care that she was revealing her feeling to him. All she cared about was holding on to him, feeling the solid reality of him. "Hold me," she pleaded. "Please hold me. Oh, Matt, I was so scared."

Matt's arms tightened, crushing her soft body against the hard strength of his own. "Ginnie, were you afraid I'd gone back in time again?"

"Yes." Virginia muffled a sob in his jacket. "When you weren't there, and I couldn't find you, I thought...I was afraid...." She shuddered.

"I'm here." The muscles in his arms flexed. "Ginnie, don't cry, honey, I'm here."

Neither of them knew how long they stood there, clinging to each other like lost and frightened children. Matt was only alerted to the chill evening air by the shiver that rippled through Virginia's body.

"You're cold," he said, drawing back to look at her. A smile tilted his lips. "Matter of fact, so am I. What are we standing out here for, when it's warm inside?"

Virginia sniffled and returned his smile. "It smells good inside, too."

"Oh, hell!" Matt exclaimed. "I forgot all about the casserole in the oven." Grasping her hand, he took off at a loping gait for the complex. Virginia was forced to run to keep up with him.

The meal was not ruined. But then, it wouldn't have mattered much if it had been. Though they picked at the food, neither Virginia nor Matt really tasted it. Their gazes were locked, and in the depths of their eyes burned the desire to appease a far greater hunger. Before his meal was half-finished, Matt pushed his plate away and stood up. Without saying a word, he held out his hand to her. Letting her fork drop to the table unnoticed, Virginia rose and placed her hand in his. Then, in silent agreement, they walked to her bedroom.

Murmuring of his need for her, Matt stopped beside her double bed and drew her into his arms. Answering his plea, Virginia offered her mouth and herself to him.

His kiss began with slow reverence but swiftly escalated to a hard, driving demand. She returned his kiss with an eagerness born of awakening passion. His hands skimmed over her with restless intent until they found and claimed her breasts. Her hands slid down the length of his arms to cover his in silent approval of his possession.

"Ginnie, Ginnie." Matt's voice was rough with desire. The trembling hands that removed her clothes were gentle. "You are so very beautiful," he whispered when the last wisp of silky material lay in a shimmering pool on the floor.

"And you are incredibly handsome," Virginia whispered back, staring with unabashed admiration at the magnificence of his naked masculinity.

She went into his arms as if it was the most natural thing in the world. They sank to the bed as one. Murmuring delicious enticements, Matt set Virginia on fire with his hands and lips and tongue. Glowing like a flame, burning only for him, she drove him on by exploring his muscled, hard body.

When he could endure no more of the sweet torture, Matt slid between the silken lure of her trembling thighs. Her soft, strong hands grasped his taut hips. Moving slowly, savoring the moment, he entered her. He frowned when he met with resistance and, arching, he thrust forward, then froze when Virginia went stiff and cried out in pain.

"Ginnie?" Matt's voice betrayed his utter astonishment. "You're a virgin?"

Virginia drew a slow breath before answering. "Yes. Is that a sin?" A hint of laughter tinged her voice.

Matt shook his head, as if in disbelief. "I hurt you—and you're making jokes?"

She smoothed her palm over the muscles contracting in his buttocks. "I'm a physician, Matt—remember? I knew what to expect." She pressed against him with her hands, drawing him deeper within her. "The pain is gone now, and the tension is easing."

Matt could feel the truth of her words. The stiffness was draining from her body, being replaced by a different, exciting tension. Passion flared anew, and again he began to move, stroking into her with gentle thrusts.

"Yes, yes!" Virginia cried, sinking her nails into his flesh as she arched to meet his advance. "Love me, Matt. Show me how very real you are!"

"I'm real, love," he said in a voice tight with strain. "You'll see." Bending to her, he pressed his open mouth to hers and matched the measured thrusts of his tongue to the increasing rhythm of his body.

Virginia felt drenched in sensation. Her body was on fire, every nerve ending burning, screaming for release from the sensual tension. She had never dreamed it could be like this...that anything could feel like this. She cried out in wonder when the tension snapped, flinging her into the depths of the shudders that were cascading through her body.

A moment later she heard Matt's muffled cry of satisfaction, and felt the rippling tremors that shook his long, muscular form. Locked together, they rode the storm wave to the tranquil shore.

"God!" Matt groaned as he levered himself onto the mattress beside her. "I've never experienced anything like that in my life." He drew several deep breaths. "That was wonderful. You're wonderful." Reaching for her, he gathered her into his arms, close to his flushed body. "I'm sorry for hurting you," he murmured, kissing her with tender concern.

"Don't be," she whispered, teasing his lower lip with the tip of her tongue. "After the initial shock, I loved every tension-filled minute of it."

Matt's roar of joyous laughter danced in the dark room. "I was wrong," he said after his laughter subsided. "You aren't wonderful, you're damned fantastic."

"I might say the same about you," Virginia responded, loving the afterglow of teasing banter. "But I don't want to risk inflating your male ego."

"My ego?" Propping himself on his forearm, Matt loomed over her. "What would you say if I told you that you were in real danger of inflating something other than my ego?"

"So soon?" Virginia stared at him in amazement. "I mean really?"

"Really," he repeated, his lips twitching with amusement. "I wasn't merely hungry for you, Ginnie. I was starved."

"Has it been such a long, dry spell for you?" she asked, innocently falling into his trap. Her eyes narrowed in suspicion when he grinned with wicked intent.

"Over a hundred years."

Nine

You devil!''

Virginia slapped her palm against his shoulder, laughed, then curled her fingers into his long hair and drew his mouth to hers.

"You angel," Matt murmured, teasing her with nibbling little kisses. "I knew you were an angel from the first moment I saw you, standing there above me, with the light shining on your hair, making a halo around your beautiful face."

"Oh, Matt." Tears rushed to her eyes, and she cradled his lean cheeks with her palms.

"I don't want to terrify you, Ginnie," he murmured, brushing his mouth back and forth over hers. "But I love you, you know, and now that I have you, I'll never let you go."

His teasing mouth was driving her crazy. Feeling herself losing control, Virginia pressed against his face, holding him still. "Matt, wait," she said when he strained forward to reach her lips. "I must tell you."

"Make it quick," he growled. "I can't wait much longer. I want to kiss you, love you."

"That's what I wanted to tell you." She was getting breathless, because his mouth was getting closer. "I love you, too. I didn't want to, but I do."

"I know you didn't want to." Breaking her hold, he gave her a quick but proper kiss. "But I thank God that you do."

His mouth claimed hers in a hungry kiss hot with renewed passion. Virginia was lost, but she didn't mind, didn't care, because she was lost inside Matt's arms, his gentle, urgent possession, his encompassing love.

Deliciously drained, they slept, Virginia's head nestled on his broad chest, Matt's arms holding her close.

Virginia woke to Matt's hand stroking her back. "What time is it?" she asked, sensuously arching into his touch.

"Who knows?" Matt replied, massaging the base of her spine. "Who cares."

Opening one eye, she peered at the digital clock on the nightstand and read the numbers aloud. "It's 7:46." She arched again, rubbing her breasts against him. "Mmm...that feels good," she murmured, nuzzling through the dark whorls of chest hair to press her mouth to his warm skin.

"So does that," he said on a sharp, indrawn breath. His big hands grasped her hips to shift her body onto his, making her aware of her effect on him. "That feels even better."

"Greedy devil, aren't you?" Virginia gasped, and moved her hips into alignment with his.

"Sure." Matt groaned his appreciation and ran one hand down the backs of her thighs. "Like I told you, it's been..."

"Over a hundred years," she finished for him, muffling her laughter against the silken mat on his chest.

Matt's laughter blended with hers, setting the tone for their lovemaking. Laughing, teasing, tickling, tormenting each other, they played an ancient male-female game. They were all over the bed—as well as one another—and at one point even rolled to the floor. Landing on the soft mound of covers, which had preceded them by some minutes, neither one felt the fall. Their laughter ceased when at last, panting from exertion and heightened passion, they joined again, two individuals fused, body, mind and soul into one.

"I'm hungry," Matt said much later. Sprawled beside her on the bed, he raised his arms and stretched like a huge, satisfied cat.

Pushing her wildly tangled hair from her face, Virginia looked at him in blank astonishment. "Already?"

"For food, woman." Matt grinned at her.

"Oh." Virginia grinned back at him.

"So what are you going to do about it?"

"Not a thing." She yawned behind her hand. "You're in charge of the kitchen, remember?"

Matt groaned. "Yeah, and it's a mess."

"Uh-huh." Virginia nodded in solemn agreement. "You could always warm up the casserole."

"Ugh," he grunted. "Aren't you hungry?"

Virginia's smile was sweet. "Not if I have to make the food myself."

"I've got you spoiled."

"And I love it."

"What about me?"

Virginia's voice went soft. "I love you, too."

"You win." Matt rolled from the bed. "I'll get a shower, then fix us something." He strode to her bathroom, then paused in the doorway to glance at her. "But you can fix the bed." Her laughter followed him into the shower.

"When did you first realize that you were falling in love with me?" Coming from Matt, the age-old lover's question sounded brand-new.

They were seated at the kitchen table. After Matt had finished in the bathroom, Virginia had showered, then stripped and remade the bed, while he cleared away the dinner remnants and cooked scrambled eggs and bacon.

"Oh, not long after I brought you here from the hospital, I guess," she replied on a sigh.

"That long?" Matt gaped at her, egg-laden fork poised near his open mouth. His movement slow, absent, he lowered the fork to his plate. "Dammit, Ginnie, I've been going crazy for three months, trying to think of a way to make you love me! Why didn't you tell me?"

"Because I didn't want to be in love with you," she answered with simple honesty.

"Because of who I am? Where I come from? The time I come from?"

"No, of course not," Virginia said in quick denial. "I didn't mean just you," she explained. "I didn't want to fall in love with any man."

"But . . . why?" Matt looked baffled.

"I tried to explain all this to you before, Matt," she said, breaking pieces off the slice of toast she was holding. "I keep a tight schedule. I never had the time or desire to rearrange my life to suit a man."

"Bull," Matt snorted rudely, startling her. He shoved back his chair and stood up. "You've kept to your schedule ever since I've been here," he pointed out. Lifting his coffee cup, he drained it, then carried it and his empty plate to the sink. When he turned to face her again, his expression was bland...too bland. "And I don't expect things to change all that much now...except that we'll be sleeping together, instead of apart."

"We will?" Virginia challenged him, arching her brows.

"You know we will." Matt smiled. "And don't try to change the subject."

"What was the subject?"

"You, and the reason you were still a virgin."

Virginia pushed away her unfinished meal for the second time that evening. "I don't know what the big deal is about my being a virgin!" she exclaimed, tossing the mangled toast onto her plate with a show of temper.

"It's about you," he said. "Finished?" He inclined his head to indicate her plate. When she nodded, he cleared her things away, and continued as if there'd been no break. "And your fear of men."

Virginia stared at him in amazement. "I'm not afraid of men. Did I act like I was afraid of you?"

"Yes, now that I think about it," Matt replied, bringing the dishcloth to wipe the table. "The first day I was here, when you told me the 'house rules,' you weren't angry, you were scared silly. Why?"

"Matt, really..." she began.

"Why, Ginnie?" he persisted, flinging the dish-cloth into the sink. "Tell me."

Virginia glared at him. He smiled with gentle patience. His smile defeated her. She sighed and moved her shoulders in an I-give-up shrug. "I don't actually fear men, Matt," she said in a soft, tired voice. "In fact, as friends, they're fine. It's simply that, ever since I was old enough to notice such things, I've seen what usually happens to women when they make the mistake of falling in love."

Matt frowned. "What does happen?"

She shrugged again. "Because his own self-image is fragile, he bolsters his ego by undermining hers. You know—Mr. Machismo and his mate. She may even earn as much money as he does, but don't forget, he is the man of the house—never mind that when the man of the house has an illness as minor as a little cold, he is more of a child than the youngest infant in the family. And so, if only to keep peace, the woman suppresses her own individuality. Over time he exerts his will until she has precious little of her own, becoming, not the full potential of her own self, but *his* wife, the mother of *his* children, *his* echo and shadow." A faint smile played at the edges of her lips.

"I decided before I was fifteen that I would never allow the same thing to happen to me. I knew what I wanted to do, what I wanted to be. And I was determined that no man would ever get the opportunity to play out his fantasy of lord and master over me."

Matt looked pensive for a moment, then grinned and said, "Lord and master, huh? The idea has appeal. I can see it all now," he went on, enlarging on the theme. "Me lounging by a roaring fire, and you, naked of course, pampering my ego, bolstering my self-image, stroking my—"

"Stuff it, Hawk," she drawled.

His laughter reverberated in the small room. "Honey, I must admit that I'm glad you were so determined to resist other men." Matt's eyes gleamed with inner amusement. "But I gotta tell you, I can't see you knuckling under to any mere male." His smile became a grin. "Hell, if I thought it might work, I'd give it a shot myself."

Virginia's smile was wry. "It wouldn't work."

"Well, isn't that what I just said?"

She nodded.

"Knew I heard it somewhere."

Virginia laughed. "Matthew Hawk, you're crazy."

"No, honey." The amused gleam vanished from his eyes, overshadowed by serious intent. "I'm just happy to be alive, and to be here...with you."

"Oh, Matt." She reached for him. He pulled her out of her chair and into his arms.

"You know, the first time I got a clear look at you, when you walked into my room Christmas afternoon,

I kinda got the idea that you were . . . well, sorta like a lady of the line.''

They were back in bed. Matt was propped against the headboard, one hand wrapped around a steaming cup of coffee, the other wrapped around Virginia.

"A what?" She lifted her head from his chest to stare at him in bewilderment.

Matt shrugged, then winced as the coffee sloshed over the rim of the cup and splashed his hand. "A lady of the line is . . . eh, well . . . something like a loose woman."

"*Something* like a loose woman?"

Matt grinned. "Okay, more like a prostitute."

"A pros—Matthew Hawk!" Virginia exclaimed. "Whatever made you think a thing like that? I...I..."

"Calm down, honey." Risking being scalded by the sloshing coffee, Matt silenced her with a kiss. It was only after his mouth claimed hers that he realized she was shaking with laughter, not fury. The kiss ended when the hot liquid seared his skin again. "Damn!" he muttered, setting the cup on the nightstand. "Now look what you made me do."

Virginia laughed into his face. "Serves you right. A lady of the line, indeed. What an expression. I love it!"

"Well, it doesn't fit you, anyway," Matt grumbled.

"Why did you ever think it did?" she asked.

He shrugged. "You were wearing paint on your face, and your legs were exposed, and I'd never in my life seen heels that high on a lady's shoes."

"Paint? Legs? Heels?" Virginia almost choked on the words, again convulsed with laughter. "Oh, Matt, that's a riot!"

"You gotta remember, I didn't know where I was." But Matt's indignant expression was ruined by the twitch at the corners of his mouth.

"And then I told you you could stay at my place!" she gasped around a fresh bout of laughter. "You must have really believed you'd died and gone to heaven!" She gave him a sparkling look. "No wonder you were so shocked at finding that I was still a virgin."

Matt's expression changed, becoming sober and concerned. "Are you hurting, Ginnie? I mean, was it too much?"

Virginia raised her hand to smooth the frown lines from his face. "I'm fine...a little tender, that's all."

"But..."

She slid her fingers over his lips. "Matt, I'm a doctor, and I've made my diagnosis. The patient will live."

"Good," Matt muttered against her fingers. "I'm glad."

That night set the precedent for the following weeks. Their days continued as they had before, with Virginia working and Matt learning and walking. But their nights had changed. Instead of sitting in front of the TV or with their noses buried in their respective books, Virginia and Matt spent the majority of their time in bed, her bed, making love and conversation— not necessarily at the same time.

The very next night conversation came first and concerned protection... Virginia's.

"Of course, I'm willing to go on the pill, but I can't start taking it until next month," she said, after explaining the various methods of birth control that were available. "So, until then..." Her voice faded as she dropped a foil-wrapped packet into his hand. "You don't mind?"

"No, I don't mind," Matt replied. He looked at the packet, then at her. His eyes were warm, glowing with love for her. "But then again, I wouldn't mind seeing my baby growing inside of you, either."

Melting, Virginia threw her arms around his neck and admitted, "Oh, Matt, I love you so much, and I'd love to feel your baby growing inside of me!"

The packet was tossed into the nightstand drawer, and the prescription for the pill remained in Virginia's purse. As was soon evident, it was already too late for either.

"I've told you most of my life story," Matt said one night the following week. "But you haven't said much at all about yourself."

Virginia almost never spoke about her past. But, snuggled against his warm body, replete and relaxed from his special brand of lovemaking, Virginia was amenable to being forthcoming, if not expansive.

"There's not much to tell," she said. "I was born and raised right here in Conifer, went to a university in Philadelphia, then came back here to finish my internship at Conifer General."

"Family?" Matt nudged, wanting more.

"I had one."

"Ginnie."

She shrugged, and heard him catch his breath as her body rubbed against his. "My parents endured a long, unhappy marriage. She was repressed. He was bored," she said in a monotone. "They finally divorced a couple of years ago. They have since both remarried. My mother now lives in California. Her husband's in real estate development. And my father lives in upper New York State. His new wife is exactly what he always wanted... an adoring doormat."

"You're bitter?"

"No," Virginia denied. "Realistic."

Matt shifted to his side to look at her. "Our marriage won't be like that, honey."

She arched her brows. "We're getting married?"

His eyes held hers. "Aren't we?"

"Yes."

"Yes," he echoed softly. He smiled, then scowled in consternation. "That is, if we can. I have no identification of any kind. How—?" he began.

Virginia interrupted him. "There are ways," she assured him. "I met all types of people while I was doing residency in Emergency. I remember one man had identification in three different names." She smiled at the memory. "He told me that if I ever needed anything, a birth certificate, whatever, I shouldn't hesitate to call him." Her smile turned rueful. "Oh, yes, there are ways... None of them legal, of course, but..." She allowed her voice to trail away.

"But we'll do what we have to do," Matt finished for her.

And they did. A week and a half later, Matt had all the identification he required, and all in his own name.

After a cold snap, spring arrived in full force. The sunshine was bright and warm. The grass turned from brown to a lush green. Buds appeared on tree limbs. Flowers burst into bloom...and so did Virginia. In late April she visited the hospital's staff obstetrician. She confirmed Virginia's self-diagnosis.

Virginia held her news close to her heart until later that night, when Matt lay beside her, exhausted and content.

"Matt?"

"Mmm?" Yawning, he pulled her into his arms.

"Do you remember the discussion we had last month about birth control?" she asked softly.

"Uh-huh." He yawned again. "Why?"

"Do you remember what you said at the time?"

Matt was quiet for a moment, thoughtful. "Yeah. I said that I didn't mind using something," he said slowly, "but that I also wouldn't mind seeing you grow—" He stopped speaking abruptly, his questioning gaze probing her eyes. "Ginnie, are you trying to tell me that you're pregnant?"

Virginia's smile was tremulous, uncertain. Her voice was little more than a whisper. "Yes."

His arms tightened, crushing her to him. "Honey, that's wonderful!" He kissed her hard, then drew back, his expression hopeful, his voice hesitant. "Isn't it?"

Virginia laughed and cried at the same time. "Yes, Matt, I think it is wonderful."

"We've got to get married," he said, suddenly wide-awake and exuberant. "The sooner the better."

"Tonight yet?" Virginia teased, smiling mistily.

"No," he answered seriously. "I've got other plans for tonight."

"Really? Like what?" she asked, certain she already knew. She was wrong.

"Like the future," Matt replied, surprising her. "I've been meaning to discuss it with you."

Virginia squirmed, working her soft curves into a comfortable position around his angles. "Okay," she said, after she'd succeeded in drawing a protesting groan from him. "I'm all ears. Discuss."

"Oh, honey," Matt muttered, gliding his hand down her back and over her hip. "Believe me, you are definitely not all ears. You're all soft, and silky, and warm, and—"

"Matthew," she cut in on him in a warning tone. "Stop feeling and start talking. Discuss."

"Nag," he groused, gliding his palm to her waist. "Anyway, I've been thinking about what I'm going to do with myself, how I'm going to support my—" he shot her a happy grin "—my growing family."

Virginia refrained from pointing out to him that she earned an excellent income and had a tidy sum saved. She knew better. Matt was a proud man. He paid his way...as he had taken great pains to inform her, when he had insisted that she keep the lion's share of the money she had gotten from the collector for his gold coins. Recalling that scene and his obstinacy, she asked with genuine interest, "Have you decided on something?"

"Yes."

She sighed with impatience. "Were you planning to tell me? Or must I guess?"

Matt laughed. "Well, first of all, I'll need some money."

"Okay," she agreed. "I have some savings. How much do you think you'll need?"

He looked astonished. "I don't want your money."

"But you just said you needed some," she reminded him in exasperation. "Why won't you take mine?"

"Because I have my own."

Ten

Your own money?" Virginia frowned. "I don't understand. I thought all you had were those gold coins."

"All I had on me at the time I was shot," Matt agreed. "But I have more."

"Gold coins?" She felt as confused as he sounded confident.

"Of course," he said. "I was always paid in gold, and I always set some of it aside."

Virginia smiled. She remembered him telling her that the coins in his belt were his pay. Assuming he was paid monthly, as was usually the case at the time, Matt had earned $275 a month. How much could he have set aside? And what had the marshal been saving for...a rainy day? Or, more likely, a wild time with the ladies of the line when he got back to town? Curious, and maybe a trifle jealous, she twined a finger into the curly mat of hair on his chest and casually asked, "Were you saving for anything in particular?"

There was nothing casual about Matt's response . . . to her query or to what her finger play was doing to his libido. "Sure," he said on a sharp breath. "But if you want to know, you'd better corral that maverick finger of yours."

She released the dark swirl at once and curled her fingers into her palm. "Sorry."

"I'm not," Matt chuckled. "But anyway, I was saving it to buy a place of my own someday in the future, after I was past it." His voice took on a dry drawl. "Of course, I never dreamed it would be this far into the future."

His answer, his odd phrasing, confused her. "What kind of place of your own? And what do you mean by 'after you were past it'? Past what?"

"Past being a mite faster than the hombre I was after," he said, splaying his hand against her ribs when she shuddered as she recalled the bullet wound in his chest. "Easy, honey. It's over, I'm alive." His voice grew lower and held a note of wonder. "Hell, being shot was the best thing that ever happened to me! It gave me you."

Virginia shuddered again. "I hate guns," she said with passion. "And I hate the thought of that gun you have hidden away in your dresser. I wish you'd get rid of it."

"Forget it." Matt's tone was flat, hard, final. "You never know when I might need it."

"Matt, this is the twentieth century!" Virginia cried. "Men no longer need to carry guns for protection."

"Yeah, I noticed that," he retorted dryly. "I can tell how protected decent folks are by all the reports in the papers and on TV about killings and muggings and rape. Forget it, honey. I'm keeping the Colt."

Virginia longed to argue further but, since he'd made a valid point, she backed away from the subject. "Tell me what kind of place you were hoping to buy."

His fingers flexed gently into her ribs in a silent gesture of appreciation of her retreat. "A small spread," Matt replied. "A place to raise horses...and babies," he added softly, sliding his hand to her still flat tummy.

"Thank you," she whispered, reciprocating by placing her palm over the back of his hand. Virginia had no idea how much a small spread would cost, but she had a depressing notion that his meager savings wouldn't be enough. "How much had you saved?" she asked, determined that Matt would have his "place," even if she had to wipe out her bank balance.

"The last time I checked, it came to a little over three thousand dollars."

Virginia jolted back, knocking his arm away from her body. "Over three thousand dollars!" she repeated in shock. "In the same kind of gold coins?"

"Exactly the same." Matt smiled.

"If you could sell them for the same amount that you got for those other coins, you could see a return of..." She broke off to do some rapid mental calculations, but was too excited to think straight, let alone count. "A bundle!"

His smile grew into a wicked grin. "Yeah, honey, that's the way I figured it."

"Matt, that's wonderful for you. I'm deligh—Oh!" she cried as she was struck by a deflating thought. "Matt, it's been over a hundred years. You don't know if your account is still on record, or even if the bank still exists."

"Bank?" Matt snorted. "Honey, you ever hear of bank robbers? I never trusted my money to a bank."

"Then where *did* you keep it?"

"Don't worry, honey," he soothed. "It's in a safe place."

Virginia sighed. "Where, Matt?"

"I stashed it in the well on that scraggly piece of land that came to me when my mother died."

"Oh, Matt." Virginia's shoulders drooped.

Coiling his arm around her, he drew her down to him again. "What's wrong, Ginnie?"

"You keep forgetting that it's been over a hundred years," she replied sadly.

"I haven't forgotten anything, honey," he murmured, brushing his mouth over her temple. "Don't worry, the money's safe. That well was built to last a lot longer than a hundred years."

"Unless someone built a high rise on top of it," she said morosely. "Or a whole town."

"Oh, hell," he muttered.

"My sentiments exactly," she concurred.

"Well, there's only one way to find out," Matt said. "I'll have to go back and see for myself."

"How are you going to do that?" Virginia asked.

"By jet?" Matt's tone held a boyish-sounding note of hope.

The 727 rolled into position on the runway. Buckled into the window seat beside Virginia, Matt's body was taut, his eyes bright with expectation.

Over two weeks had passed since the night he had stated his decision to return to Texas. Matt had wanted to leave at once but, as Virginia was adamant about going with him, they had been forced to wait until she could arrange her schedule to allow her to take time off.

The jet engines revved and the plane moved forward, gathering speed as it dashed down the runway. The long fingers clasped around Virginia's tightened with heightened tension when the plane left the ground, seeming to rise straight up into the cloudless sky.

"Damn," Matt breathed. "This is great."

Sharing the experience with Matt made the flight as adventurous and exciting for Virginia as her first air trip had been. Observing him, loving him, she suddenly realized that she had been reexperiencing many aspects of life during the previous months. She was seeing everything through his eyes, and finding it all new and exciting.

When the plane reached altitude and leveled off, Virginia settled back to relax for the remainder of what she knew would be a relatively boring flight.

Matt wasn't bored, he was interested in everything. He plied Virginia with questions and he even enjoyed the in-flight meal, eating every bit of his own and half of hers. Fortunately, the descent and landing were made smoothly, although Virginia doubted that Matt would have noticed if they hadn't been, since his nose was pressed against the window.

Matt was amazed by the crowds of travelers and the hustle and bustle of Dallas-Fort Worth airport, and stunned by his first close look at a city. Seated beside Virginia in the rental car that she had arranged to have waiting for them, his head swiveled from side to side as she drove the beltway around Dallas, before heading for Fort Worth.

Despite the obvious changes, Matt recognized Fort Worth, if only because the famous stockyards were still there. Like any other tourist, he admired the bronze statue of Texas longhorns and a cattleman sculpted by T. D. Kelsey. But he was quiet and withdrawn as they strolled along Exchange Avenue.

"It must all seem rather strange to you now," Virginia murmured, indicating the shops lining the street with a wave of her hand.

"Yeah, it looks a lot different from my old stomping grounds." He nodded, then he grinned at her. "It's a whole lot cleaner, too." With a final glance around, he grasped her hand and strode off in the direction of the parking area. "I've seen enough," he said. "Let's go get my money."

Finding the small ranch proved easier than Virginia had feared it would be. After he studied a detailed map he'd purchased in one of the tourist shops, Matt pinpointed the section, located some distance southwest of Dallas. He told her when to turn off the highway onto a secondary road, and when to turn off that onto a back road. Then, with the instincts of a natural tracker, he told her to turn onto a narrow dirt road that was barely visible.

"You just drive nice and slow along here for a mile or so," Matt said, narrowly studying the terrain. "I'll tell you when to stop."

When he gave the word, Virginia braked the car, then sat staring at the barren bleakness of the landscape. This scrap of nothing was his heritage? she thought, aching with love and compassion for him.

"It's a real mess, isn't it?" Matt observed, correctly reading her expression. "And that mess killed my father and mother." Sighing, he pushed open the car door. "The sight of it churns my gut. Let's find my money and get out of here."

Virginia had to step lively to keep up with Matt's determined stride. At a near trot, she followed in his wake as he skirted the remnants of a collapsed building, then jumped, startled when he let out a sudden loud shout.

"Eu-re-ka! What'd I tell ya, honey?" he yelled. "Hurry over here and look. The well's still here."

And there it was. Panting, Virginia stared at the round, foot-wide stone wall. Parts of the wall were crumbling, but it was still there. Fascinated, she watched as Matt moved unerringly to a spot in the wall that looked to her like any other. She caught her breath when he sank to his haunches, and gnawed her lower lip as he worked one large rock, jiggling it back and forth until he could pull it free.

"Now pray," Matt said, slanting a grin at her over his shoulder as he inserted his hand into the hollow.

Excitement and hope making her feel slightly sick, Virginia kept her gaze riveted to the wall. She gasped aloud when Matt withdrew his hand. His fingers were wrapped around the top of a bulging, soft buckskin pouch. He repeated the process three times; she gasped each time he did it. By the time he had examined the pouches, she felt exhausted.

"It's all here," he informed her, exhaling deeply. "Just as I left it over a hundred years ago."

"Now you can have that place you wanted," Virginia said, blinking against a surge of hot tears.

"Yes." Walking to her, Matt drew her into his arms. "Now I can raise horses . . . and babies."

Virginia went absolutely still, for in that instant the moment of truth, her moment of truth was upon her. From the time she was old enough to make her own decisions, she had known that the one thing she didn't want was a commitment to a man, any man. When Matt had talked about his own place before, the idea was nebulous, contingent upon the reality of the gold he had stashed away. Now the gold was real, she had seen it, and Matt was no longer talking about a neb-ulous hope but about a definite place, somewhere to raise horses and babies. . . . Matt was talking commit-ment.

Could she handle it? The thought flashed through Virginia's mind as she gazed into his shining blue eyes. She was carrying his child, but her pregnancy alone did not imply commitment; Virginia was confident of her ability to cope with the rigors of single parent-hood. No, the fact of the child growing inside her body had little bearing on her deliberations. The single as-pect she had to deal with was whether or not she could agree to a commitment with this man.

A shadow of uncertainty flickered in Matt's eyes, dimming the bright light of expectancy. A line of consternation drew his dark brows together. A pang tugged at Virginia's emotions. No one she had ever met frowned quite like Matt. Come to that, she suddenly realized, no one, no man she had ever met did anything or was anything quite like Matt.

Matt was definitely a man of his own time—a confusing, exasperating, delightful mixture of hidden tenderness and obvious toughness. He had adapted extraordinarily well to his strange new environment, yet had retained a certain quality that set him apart from other men. Virginia knew without a shred of doubt that Matt would always be the man he had been over a hundred years before. He would grow—she had already seen the beginning of that growth. He would deepen in emotional understanding—the process had already begun. But basically she knew that Matt would always be Matt, a man confident in his identity and comfortable with his own masculinity, a man secure within himself.

And in that instant, Virginia intuitively knew that this man was perhaps the only one she could ever make a commitment with. She was head over heels in love with him, but in addition to that she felt instinctively that they were soul mates, destined to be together. Matthew Hawk had traveled through time and space to be with her. She was as exclusively his as he was obviously hers.

Her fears resolved, Virginia was almost afraid to ask the only question left in her mind, afraid of hearing his answer, but she had to know. "Where? I mean, did you have any place special in mind."

"Well, I had kinda taken a fancy to the foothills near the Anaconda Mountains of Montana."

Virginia's spirits nose-dived. But he wasn't finished. Lifting her chin with one finger, Matt smiled at her in tender understanding.

"But foothills are foothills," he murmured. "And the foothills surrounding Conifer, Pennsylvania suit me just fine." He arched his brows. "How about you?"

Tears of relief and happiness rolling down her cheeks, Virginia whispered, "They suit me just fine, too."

"Good." Lowering his head, Matt kissed her tear-wet eyes, her damp cheeks and trembling lips. When he raised his head, his eyes were once again smiling, bright with purpose, alive. "Let's go home."

Virginia and Matt were married the Saturday after they returned to Conifer from Texas. With no fuss, no fanfare, but a wealth of love, they exchanged their vows in a civil ceremony. Holed up in Virginia's bedroom they had a one-day honeymoon, and then she went back to work.

Matt's gold coins were sold before spring gave way to summer, portioned out to a dozen eager and rich private collectors. His profit was, as Virginia had aptly predicted, "A bundle."

They spent almost all of Virginia's free time driving around the foothills, looking at property offered for sale. Most of the prospects were either too large or too run-down. There were two that Virginia considered workable, but shaking his head, Matt held firm in his belief that he'd know the place when he found it.

Late in August, becoming discouraged, they made a Sunday appointment to look at a small farm. The location was perfect for Virginia, since it was fifteen minutes from her office and the hospital. In fact, from the realtor's description, the property sounded entirely too good to be true. To her surprise, the farm was everything the realtor claimed it to be and more. Set in a valley nestled at the base of the foothills, the farm was a beautiful piece of real estate.

Virginia fell in love with it at once. Her eyes shining, she looked at Matt, and saw the emotion she was feeling gleaming in his blue eyes.

"It'll need some fixing up," he said laconically.

"Well, if you'd rather not bother..." Virginia let her voice trail away, as if she really didn't care.

Laughing, Matt swept her into his arms. "It's ours, and you know it." Planting a hard kiss upon her smiling mouth, he promised, "I'll have it ready by the time the baby comes."

Virginia had never really believed it was possible to be so happy. She had an ardent, caring husband who, from all indications, had no problem whatever with his self-image—Matt was all male in the best definition of the word. She was healthy and enjoying her pregnancy. She was working, and since the baby wasn't due until after Christmas, she planned to keep working until Thanksgiving. She was content.

By the time summer surrendered to fall with a blaze of color, Matt had completed all the renovations in the farmhouse except for the natural stone fireplace he was installing in the living room. The glorious leaves withered and drifted to the ground as the wide stone chimney climbed up the living-room wall to the ceiling.

After Thanksgiving, Virginia went on maternity leave . . . and on a shopping spree. While Matt worked around the house, she shopped for things to make it feel like a home.

It was during one such shopping expedition, this one for Christmas presents for Matt, that Virginia stopped by a used bookstore on her way back to the apartment. Throughout the eleven months that had passed since Matt had appeared, Virginia had continued to search for books on the subject of time travel. She had visited the shop before, and so went directly to the section where the books dealing with all forms of paranormal material were kept.

Virginia examined several paperback books before noticing a slim hardcover volume stuck between two hefty tomes. The title—*Here and Gone*—was scripted in faded gilt on the spine. Intrigued, she removed the book and opened it at the preface. She began to tremble as her eyes skimmed the three paragraphs of information. The book was a compilation of ten separate instances of what could only be explained as actual accounts of travel through time. Excitement curling through her, Virginia paid for the book, then rushed home to read it.

Several hours later, when Virginia closed the book, her happiness was shattered and her contentment gone. Though she tried to reject the conclusions drawn by the journalist who had compiled the accounts, uncertainty had been instilled into her mind.

Though each of the ten instances covered in the book had taken place at different times and in a vari-

ety of places, there were similarities in every one of
them. The journalist had garnered the information in
ten states along the eastern seaboard. The accounts
concerned the sudden and unexplained appearance of
ten different people, some male, some female, all of
whom were reportedly disoriented and confused, in-
sisting that they were not where they should be. In
eight of the cases, the people claimed to be from a
former time period. In the other two, they maintained they were from the future. The journalist stated
that in every case the people were tested by experts in
the proper fields and declared healthy and fit in mind
and body. Further, the author maintained that in every
instance, the person involved disappeared again—exactly one year later.

Matt came home late in the afternoon to find Virginia sitting in a corner of the sofa, pale and trembling.

"Ginnie?" Dropping to his knees on the floor beside her, Matt stared into her frightened eyes. "Honey,
what's wrong? Is it the baby? Are you in pain?"

"No, no." Virginia shook her head. "I'm...it's this
book, Matt." She thrust the slim volume into his
hands. "Read it, Matt. Then, please, please, tell me
it's all a fake, that it's not true."

"A book?" Matt frowned. "Honey, what is this?"

"Just read it, Matt, and then we'll talk."

But they didn't talk after he had finished reading,
not really. They denied, derided and rationalized, but
didn't really talk, not verbally. But they communi-
cated with their eyes, and in those depths was revealed the uncertainty and terror that lurked in their
hearts.

By mutual agreement, Virginia and Matt decided not to move into their new home until after the baby was born. The reason they gave each other for the delay was the closeness of her apartment to the hospital. But they both knew the real reason.

It began snowing around dawn the day before Christmas. Virginia went into labor late in the afternoon. The apparent coincidence in the time frame terrified her, though Matt was by her side every minute, coaching, encouraging, soothing, even joking with her. Only his eyes betrayed the fear he refused to let show or give voice to.

At 10:25 p.m. their daughter came into the world, squalling loudly against the indignity of it all. Exhausted, eyelids drooping, Virginia clung to Matt's hand.

"I love you so much," she whispered in a cry from the heart. "Don't leave. Please, don't leave me."

"I won't." Matt's voice was hoarse from strain. "You know I could never leave you. You're my life."

Virginia was half-asleep when she heard him begin to murmur. "I love you, Ginnie. Thank you for my daughter. She's beautiful, like her mother. Take care of her for me, if I . . ."

Matt's voice trailed away. Virginia was asleep.

Feeling the need to be alone, just in case he should do a disappearing act, Matt walked beside the litter that transported Virginia to her room, saw her settled into bed, then turned and walked to the visitors' lounge.

The room was empty. A partially finished puzzle was set out on a card table. Matt stared at the scattered pieces and sighed. It all looked so normal, so permanent. He was tired, and he was scared. Dropping into a chair by the window, he folded his arms on the wide windowsill and stared at the shimmering snowflakes dancing in the air.

In memory, Matt relived the events of his year in the twentieth century. Within that one short year he had seen and done things never dreamed of in his own time. And yet the most important event of all was something that had been happening through all time.

He had found love.

Leaning forward, Matt rested his head upon his folded arms and closed his eyes. It was Christmas Eve, almost Christmas morning. Within one short year, everything he had wanted had come to him. He had a decent life. He had a beautiful new daugher. He had Virginia's love.

A woman of his own.

Had he found it all, only to lose it again? Praying for Virginia, for their child and for himself, Matt fell asleep.

He wakened to the sound of church bells celebrating the arrival of Christmas. They sounded exactly like the ones he'd heard ringing from the crest of a hill in Montana. For an instant Matt was afraid to open his eyes. He flexed his fingers. They scraped against a hard surface, not cold snow. Drawing a deep breath, he raised his head and opened his eyes.

He was not lying on the ground in a pool of his own blood. It was Christmas morning. He was in the hospital's visitors' lounge. The year was up. He was alive. *He was no longer a stranger.*

Virginia.

Springing from the chair, Matt strode along the quiet hospital corridor to her room. He entered cautiously, so as not to disturb her. She was awake, and she was crying.

"Ginnie!" Crossing the room at a run, Matt sat down on the edge of the bed and lifted her into his arms.

"Matt! Oh, Matt!" Clinging to him, she sobbed against his chest. "I was so frightened. I thought you were gone...that you had disappeared, gone back."

"I know." Tears trailing down his cheeks, Matt held her close and murmured a silent prayer of thanks. "But I'm here, and I'm going to stay. Merry Christmas, honey. I'm home."

Epilogue

Virginia paused in the archway, a smile curving her lips as she skimmed a glance around the living room. It presented an attractive picture, not unlike those found on Christmas cards. A cheery fire crackled in the huge stone fireplace in the wall opposite her. The mantelpiece was festooned with garlands of deep green holly. Standing before the large window in the front wall was the enormous tree that Matt had dragged into the house earlier that week. The tree's decorations glistened and shimmered with dozens of white lights. Beyond the window, drifting snowflakes sparkled in the glow from the tree lights.

Dressed in tight jeans and bronzed male skin, Matt was sitting on the floor near the tree, the fingers of one hand toying with the gold bow on the small, gift-wrapped package he held in the palm of his other hand. As if sensing her presence, he looked up and smiled.

"All quiet?"

"Yes, finally," Virginia said, moving into the room. "But for a minute there, I was beginning to think Amanda would never settle for the night."

"Give the kid a break, it's her birthday." Matt grinned, and ran a slow, appreciative glance over the filmy red negligee Virginia was wearing. It was a gift from him. "On second thought," he murmured, "come down here and give me a break. You look sexy as hell in that thing."

"Talk about sexy," Virginia retorted softly, sinking to the braided carpet beside him, "you forgot to wear your shirt."

Matt's grin grew wicked. "I didn't forget it."

"That's what I thought."

"I have a present for you."

Virginia smiled. "That's what I thought."

Laughing, Matt leaned forward to give her a quick kiss. "That present comes later," he murmured. "This one comes first." He placed the small package in her palm.

"But Matt," she protested. "You've already given me this gown, and it's only Christmas Eve."

"This one's special, in honor of the occasion," he said mysteriously. "Go on, open it."

Her curiosity aroused, Virginia carefully removed the bow and wrapping paper, then raised the lid of the black velvet jeweler's case. "Oh, Matt!" she whispered, tears filling her eyes as she stared at the gleaming piece of gold that nestled in the white satin lining the case. With trembling fingers she lifted the coin from its bed, murmuring again when she saw that the coin, bearing the date 1889, had been rimmed with gold and hung on a gold chain. "Oh, darling, thank you. It's beautiful. I love it. And I love you."

Drawing her into his arms, Matt kissed the tears from her cheeks. "You're welcome," he whispered. "And now we can get to the best present of all." Laughing, he lowered her to the floor. "Just in case I haven't told you often enough, let me show you how much I love you."

From the far corner of the room, the grandfather clock struck the hour of midnight, announcing Christmas with its bell-like chimes.

Matt's mouth claimed Virginia's, and the last thing she saw before her eyes drifted shut was the solitary decoration on the wide stone chimney above the mantelpiece.

Hanging from a hook painted gold was a worn leather gun belt, complete with a Colt Peacemaker.

*   *   *   *   *

SILHOUETTE

Desire™

**Just when you thought all the good men
had gotten away along comes...**

MAN OF THE MONTH 1990

From January to December, you will once again have the chance to go wild with Desire *and* with each *Man of the Month*—twelve heart-stopping new heroes created by twelve of your favorite authors.

Man of the Month 1990 kicks off with FIRE AND RAIN by Elizabeth Lowell. And as the year continues, look for winning love stories by Diana Palmer, Annette Broadrick, Ann Major and many more.

You can be sure each and every *Man of the Month* is just as dynamic, masterful, intriguing, irritating and sexy as before. These truly are men you'll want to get to know...and *love*.

So don't let these perfect heroes out of your sight. Get out there and find your man!

MOM90-1

Silhouette Romances

Diana Palmer brings you an Award of Excellence title... and the first Silhouette Romance DIAMOND JUBILEE book.

ETHAN
by Diana Palmer

This month, Diana Palmer continues her bestselling LONG, TALL TEXANS series with *Ethan*—the story of a rugged rancher who refuses to get roped and tied by Arabella Craig, the one woman he can't resist.

The Award of Excellence is given to one specially selected title per month. Spend January with *Ethan* #694... a special DIAMOND JUBILEE title... only in Silhouette Romance.

Ethan-1

SILHOUETTE DESIRE™
presents
AUNT EUGENIA'S TREASURES
by CELESTE HAMILTON

Liz, Cassandra and Maggie are the honored recipients of Aunt Eugenia's heirloom jewels…but Eugenia knows the real prizes are the young women themselves. Read about Aunt Eugenia's quest to find them everlasting love. Each book shines on its own, but together, they're priceless!

Available in December:
THE DIAMOND'S SPARKLE (SD #537)

Altruistic Liz Patterson wants nothing to do with Nathan Hollister, but as the fast-lane PR man tells Liz, love is something he's willing to take *very* slowly.

Available in February:
RUBY FIRE (SD #549)

Impulsive Cassandra Martin returns from her travels…ready to rekindle the flame with the man she never forgot, Daniel O'Grady.

Available in April:
THE HIDDEN PEARL (SD #561)

Cautious Maggie O'Grady comes out of her shell…and glows in the precious warmth of love when brazen Jonah Pendleton moves in next door.

SD-AET-1R

Indulge a Little
Give a Lot

An irresistible opportunity to pamper yourself with free gifts (plus proofs-of-purchase and postage and handling) and help raise up to $100,000.00 for **Big Brothers/Big Sisters Programs and Services** in Canada and the United States.

Each specially marked "Indulge A Little" Harlequin or Silhouette book purchased during October, November and December contains a proof-of-purchase that will enable you to qualify for luxurious gifts. And, for every specially marked book purchased during this limited time, Harlequin/Silhouette will donate 5¢ toward **Big Brothers/Big Sisters Programs and Services**, for a maximum contribution of $100,000.00.

For details on how you can indulge yourself, look for information at your favorite retail store or send a self-addressed stamped envelope to:

INDULGE A LITTLE
P.O. Box 618
Fort Erie, Ontario
L2A 5I3

ONE PROOF OF PURCHASE

To collect your free gift you must include the necessary number of proofs-of-purchase, plus postage and handling, along with the offer certificate available in retail stores or from the above address.

CSD-3

Harlequin®/Silhouette®